William Black

Highland Cousins

A Novel: Vol. I.

William Black

Highland Cousins
A Novel: Vol. I.

ISBN/EAN: 9783337041229

Printed in Europe, USA, Canada, Australia, Japan

Cover: Foto ©Andreas Hilbeck / pixelio.de

More available books at **www.hansebooks.com**

HIGHLAND COUSINS

A Novel

BY

WILLIAM BLACK

AUTHOR OF

"A PRINCESS OF THULE," "MACLEOD OF DARE," ETC., ETC.

IN THREE VOLUMES.

VOL. I.

LONDON:

SAMPSON LOW, MARSTON & COMPANY

LIMITED,

St. Dunstan's House,

FETTER LANE, FLEET STREET, E.C.

1894.

LONDON:
PRINTED BY WILLIAM CLOWES AND SONS, LIMITED,
STAMFORD STREET AND CHARING CROSS.

CONTENTS OF VOL. I.

HIGHLAND COUSINS.

CHAPTER I.

A CONVOY.

AWAY out at the edge of the world, facing the wild Atlantic seas, a small and black procession was striving hard to make headway against a blinding gale of rain and sleet. First came a horse and cart, and in the cart was a young woman, seated on a sack of straw, and wrapped up in a thick blue-green tartan shawl that in a measure protected her from the driving gusts; then followed a straggling company of middle-aged men, their figures pitched forward against the wind, their teeth clenched, the salt spindrift dripping from shaggy eyebrows and beard, while now and again the tail-end of a plaid, escaping from the clutch of frozen fingers,

would go flying aloft in the air. Occasionally
one of the men, from mere force of habit,
would stop for a moment to try to light his
pipe; but even if his horny palms were
sufficient to shelter the sulphur match, the
wet tobacco would not burn, and the pipe
was mechanically returned to its owner's
pocket. There were two or three collies,
trotting by the side of their respective
masters; but what with the drenching showers
and the bewilderment of the tumultuous
waves, there was not a snap or a snarl left
amongst them.

At length, however, the road the travellers
were following, which hitherto had wound
along the shore, struck inland; and at this
corner stood a solitary and dismal-looking
habitation. There was no sign of any kind
to denote that here was offered entertainment
for either man or beast; but no doubt the
company knew the place; for as with one
accord they left the highway and thronged
into the narrow passage, pressing and jostling
against each other. All of them, that is to
say, except one—an elderly man, of respectable appearance, who seemed to hesitate about
leaving the girl in the cart.

"Will you not come down, Barbara," said

he, addressing her in the Gaelic tongue, "and step into the house?"

The young girl with the dark-blue Highland eyes and raven-black hair merely shook her head.

"Then will I bring you out a dram," said he, "or a piece of oatcake and cheese?"

"I am not wishing for anything," she answered, also speaking in Gaelic; and thereupon the elderly shepherd, considering himself relieved of present responsibility, followed his companions into the inn.

Apparently it was but a cold welcome they had received. There seemed to be no one about; nor was there any fire in the grate of this bare, damp-smelling, comfortless chamber into which they had crowded themselves. But they did not appear to mind much; all the pent-up speech suppressed by the storm had now broken loose; and there was a confused and high-surging babblement about funeral expenses—arrears of rent—the sale of stock—the intentions of the factor—and what not; all of them talking at once, and at cross-purposes; contradicting, asseverating, with renewed striking of matches and sucking of difficult pipes. Indeed, so vehement and vociferous was the hubbub that

when a timid-looking young lass of about
fourteen came along, bearing before her a
shovel-full of burning peats, she could hardly
win attention, until one of them called
out—

"Make way for the lass there! Come in,
Isabel. And where is your mother and the
whiskey?"

"My mother is not so well to-day," the girl
replied, as she put the peats in the grate.

"But you can get us the whiskey?" was
the instant and anxious inquiry.

"Oh, yes, indeed."

"Then make haste and bring it to us, for
there is more warmth in a glass of whiskey
than in all the peats in the island."

"And have you any oatcake in the house?"
asked another.

"No, there is no oatcake in the house," the
lass made answer. "It is at this very moment
that my grandmother is baking."

She left the room, and shortly returned
with a tray on which were ranged a number
of thick tumblers and measures, the latter
filled with a dull straw-coloured fluid; whereupon each man apportioned his own and paid
for the same. There was no drinking of
healths, for they had come away from a

solemn occasion; but this additional stimulant, following previous and liberal potations, awoke a fresh enthusiasm of eager speech—about pasture land and arable, the Crofters' Commission, the price of calves, and similar things. And perhaps it was to rebuke them that Lauchlan MacIntyre the shoemaker, a tall gaunt man of melancholy mien, pushed his way through and placed his fist on the table, the better to steady himself.

"A shame it is," he said, in Gaelic that might have been fluent if it had not been interrupted by apprehensions of hiccough—"A shame it is—that we should be talking of such worldly matters. Ay, ay, indeed, when we should be mourning with our friend—mourning—as Rachel—mourning, and refusing to be comforted. It is this day that my heart is sore for Donald Maclean—that has seen the last of his family put away from him into the earth. A fine lass she was—ay, ay, indeed, not a handsomer in these islands—and a handy and a useful creature about the croft; but we are as the grass that perisheth and the flower that withereth; and Donald—Donald will be a sorrowful man—when he finds himself among the folk of Duntroone—so that the saying will be fulfilled that was written : 'Sad is—the lowing—of a cow—on a strange pasture '——"

He tilted forward : but he did not fall ; for a powerful pair of hands had got hold of him by the shoulders, and he was dragged away from the table, and thrown unceremoniously into a corner. The elderly shepherd, who had thus interfered, and who was about the only one of them with any remaining pretensions to sobriety, now addressed him with bitter scorn :

" Yes, you are the fine man to have your wits and judgment in such a state. You do not know that it is Donald Maclean that we have been burying ; you do not know that his daughter is alive and well, and waiting for us outside in the cart ; you do not know it is she who is going to Duntroone. And you are the fine man to have the charge of her : sure I am you will be in a drunken sleep as soon as you get on board the steamer——"

" Let be—let be," said Lauchlan, fumbling in his pocket for his pipe. " I am not for quarrelling. I am a peaceable man. Duncan, have you a match ? "

" A match ! " exclaimed the other, with disdain. " Is it nothing you can think of but whiskey and tobacco ?— "

"Whiskey?" repeated Lauchlan, with an amazing alertness. "Well, now, it is your head that has the good sense in it, Duncan, sometimes—and that is the Bible's truth. And I say what you say; another good glass of whiskey will do us no harm, since we have to walk across the island to Kilree. Oh, yes, do not fear; I will look after the young lass and her father; I will take them safely to Duntroone. Have you a match, Duncan?"

The older man did not answer.

"It is I that must try to get a glass of milk for Barbara," he said to himself, as he moved away, "if there is no oatcake in the house."

But meanwhile Lauchlan—Long Lauchlan the shoemaker he was called in Duntroone on the mainland—Lauchie, while fumbling about for his pipe, had come upon a Jew's-harp; and this was a new inspiration. With heroic endeavour he struggled to his feet; he balanced himself; he placed the instrument to his lips; and began to play, in a thin, quavering strain, 'Lord Lovat's Lament. Nay, he affected to give himself something of the airs of a piper; in the limited space at his command, he paced backwards and forwards, with slow and solemn steps; there was an inward look on his face, as if he was forgetful, or disdainful, of these vain roysterers. Moreover, there was a kind of nebulous grandeur about the tall and melancholy figure; for since ever the peats had been put in the grate, the wind had been steadily blowing down the chimney, and now the apartment was thick with smoke—peat-smoke and tobacco-smoke combined; so that the performer, with his slow, funereal steps of about three inches in length, was as the dark ghost of a piper, moving to and fro unheeded and apart. And he might very well have been left to his harmless diversion; but that was not to be. In spite of the din, the tremulous, wiry sound of the Jew's-harp had caught the ear of a huge red-bearded drover from Mull who was on the other side of the table; and for some reason or another he became irritated.

"You there, Long Lauchlan," he called, "why do you play that foolish thing? If the Free Church will not let you play the pipes, a man who is a man at all would refuse to play on any instrument! It is the great piper you are—with a child's toy at your mouth!"

The piper—or harper, rather—paused,

advanced to the table, steadied himself, and fixed his gaze on his enemy.

"What—is it you say—about the Free Church?" he demanded, with his small black eyes beginning to glitter.

"This it is I am saying," responded the big red-bearded giant, with his brows lowering ominously, "that when the Free Church will be for putting down the pipes throughout the islands, then the man is not a man, but a dog every inch of him, who will give up the pipes and take in the place of the pipes what is allowed him, and that is the low, pitiful, vile toy-instrument you have there."

"Then you are a liar," said the shoemaker, with decision.

"I am a liar?" repeated the other, in an access of fury. "But you are worse, for you are a son of the devil and a liar besides—and I will smash your d——d Free Church toy!"

He made a sudden snatch across the table, caught the Jew's-harp out of the shoemaker's hand, and dashed it on the floor, dancing on it with his heavy-nailed boots. Then the tumult began. The shoemaker would get round the table. His friends held him back.

He broke away, with imprecations, and howls of rage. The drover—Red Murdoch —equally frantic, was desperately striving to dispossess himself of those who clung to him or who bravely interposed themselves between the two combatants; while random blows on both sides did nothing worse, so far, than beat the air. But what portended evil was that the angry passions thus aroused showed a tendency to become general. There were excited cries and remonstrances—the invariable prelude of a faction fight. And then, as it chanced, by some accidental swaying of the crowd, the table went over— went over with a *breenge* fit to wake the dead: the tray, the glasses, the measures, the unnecessary water-bottle hurling themselves into the little black fire-place.

It was in the midst of all this indescribable uproar that a new figure suddenly appeared on the scene—an old woman with unkempt silver-white locks and visage of terrible import. She came in quickly; she was armed with the rolling-pin she had been using at the bake-board; and with some strange sort of instinct she seemed to make straight for the two chief offenders.

"What is this, now," she exclaimed, in

shrill Gaelic, "what is this going on, and my daughter lying ill! Out with you, you drunken savages! Out of the house with you, you heathen crew!—ay, every one of you!—out of the house with you!—out!— out!—" And these panting ejaculations were accompanied by strokes so energetic and unexpected that a universal bewilderment and confusion instantly prevailed. No man's person, nor any part of it, however inferior, was safe from this merciless weapon; though it was mainly on the Mull drover and on the astonished shoemaker that her valiant belabouring fell.

"In the name of God, woman, have peace!" cried one of them.

But there was no peace—there was war— war implacable and ferocious— war that ended in a decisive victory; for in an incredibly short space of time she had driven forth the whole invertebrate crowd of them, and slammed-to the outer door. They found themselves in the rain, they hardly knew how or why. They regarded each other, as if something had occurred, that they were trying to recollect. Then their eyes fell upon the cart. The young lass was still patiently waiting there, the thick blue-green

shawl not entirely confining the tags of
raven-black hair that had been loosened by
the storm. And then Duncan the shepherd
—choosing to ignore this wild thing that had
just happened—said discreetly :

" We'd better be getting on, lads. It
would be a great pity if we were to miss
the *Sanda*."

They now followed the road that cut
across the island ; and a dismal road it was—
leading through sombre wastes of swampy
peat-moss and half-frozen tarns ; with rarely
a symptom of life anywhere, except the
occasional clanging-by overhead of a string
of wild-swans on their way to the western
seas. But at any rate the rain had stopped ;
and the wind, instead of being dead ahead,
was now on their quarter, as a sailor might
say ; so that they made very good progress—
Lauchie the shoemaker clinging on to the
tail-end of the cart, and talking to himself
the while.

As the day waned, of a sudden they
encountered the strangest sound—a long-
protracted wail that rose and fell, as if it
were some spirit of the dusk in immeasurable pain.

" May the Good Being save us, but what

is that!" was the pious ejaculation of one of
the company.

Lauchie, holding on to the cart, and still
talking to himself, laughed and chuckled.

"Oh, you are the clever boys, and no
mistake!" he said, without looking at them.
"You are the clever ones, that would squeeze
paraffin oil out of the peat; and you would
make your own sheep-dip; and you would
write to the Queen complaining of the Commission and the rents. And yet you do
not know the new steam-whistle—you have
never heard the siren steam-whistle before
—and the *Sanda* has given you a splendid
fright!—"

"The *Sanda!*" exclaimed a neighbour in
dismay, and inadvertently he relapsed into
English. "Is she *unn?*"

"Ay, she's unn," responded Lauchie,
giggling to himself, "and very soon she'll
be off again, and we'll hef to tek Barbara
Maclean ahl the weh back to Knockalanish."

But this dire threat stimulated them; they
pushed ahead, and urged on the ancient
animal in the shafts; and ere long they
came in sight of the eastern shores of the
island—with the strip of cottages called

Kilree—the bay—the rude quay and landing-slip—and, lying some few hundred yards out, a stumpy one-funnelled steamer that was again sending forth its alarming call. And was not yonder the last boat already left? They waved their plaids; they whistled; some of them ran—and one of them fell, and picked himself up again. The end of it was that the horse and cart were stopped at the top of the beach; the young lass was helped to descend; the foremost two or three of the company, hurrying along, had become possessed of a boat lying by the slip; and when Barbara Maclean and her modest bundle had been deposited in the stern, the promiscuous crew unloosed the painter, shoved off the bow, plunged their oars into the water, and proceeded to pull away with a desperate resolution to overtake the departing steamer.

They pulled and they pulled and they pulled; and they were men of strength and sinew; the oars creaked and groaned in the thole-pins. They tugged and they strained and they splashed—heads down and teeth clenched; they put their shoulders into the work with a will; they would have cheered but that they dared not waste their breath;

and again came a long howl from the *Sanda*
to encourage them—doubtless she had perceived them through the gathering dusk,
and might be disposed to grant them a few
moments of grace.

But at this moment an appalling thing
occurred. Long Lauchie the shoemaker,
who had roused himself from his placid
acquiescence of the last hour or two, and
was now madly and heroically pulling stroke,
chanced to raise his head—and behold there
was some phantasmal object confronting his
bleared eyes.

"Aw, God," he cried, terror-stricken, "we
have pulled the quay away with us!"

For there, undoubtedly, was the landing-
slip, not a dozen yards off! And the beach,
and the cottages—just above—were these
also phantoms in the twilight? Surely they
could not have hauled the whole island after
them, out into the deep?

Then came one running down to the shore,
gesticulating, shouting.

"There's a line astern! The boat's tied
astern, man! Throw off the line!"

And at last it dawned upon Lauchie's
dimly-rotating brain that the boat must have
been moored both fore and aft alongside the

slip—that they had only released the painter
at the bow—and that all their frantic pulling
had gone for nothing : in point of fact they
had not moved a yard beyond the length of
this still attaching line. So blindly and
mechanically he undid the rope from the
iron ring, and cast it into the water ; then
he resumed his place and his strenuous work
—this time with considerably less weight
dragging behind. And in due course they
reached the steamer ; the young lass, Long
Lauchie, and Red Murdoch from Mull got on
board ; the others returned with the boat
to the shore. And thus it was that Barbara
Maclean left her native island to seek a
home among her relatives in Duntroone.

CHAPTER II.

A POOR STUDENT.

The aunt of this Barbara Maclean kept a tobacconist's shop in Campbell Street, which is the main thoroughfare in the small sea-side town of Duntroone; and one evening Mrs. Maclean and her daughter Jess were seated in the parlour behind the shop, from which, through a window in the intervening door, they could observe when any customer entered. Mrs. Maclean was a spruce and trim little body, fresh-complexioned, grey-haired, and bright and alert of look; her daughter Jessie, or Jess as she was called by her intimates, was a young woman of about twenty, flaxen-haired and freckled, of pleasant features and expression, and with grey eyes, ordinarily tranquil and kindly, that could on occasion show themselves merry and humorous enough, not to say malicious.

For the rest, this was quite a snug and
cheerful apartment on so cold a night; a
brisk coal-fire was burning in the grate ; a
kettle simmered on the hob ; and there were
tea-things on the table.

"Ay," said the little Highland widow, as
she continued busy with her knitting-needles,
"it's a sad thing for a young lass to be left
dissolute in the world——"

"Desolate, mother!" Jess said, impatiently, for her mother's happy carelessness of
speech was at times a source of considerable embarrassment when neighbours were
about.

"Ay, jist that," the widow said, contentedly, "it's a sad thing for a young lass
to be left dissolute.   But it's no so bad when
she has friends to turn to ; and I'm sure
when Barbara Maclean comes to us, there will
not be a pennyworth of grudging in her
welcome.   No, no, my sister and me we had
our quarrels in the old days ; but my sister's
lass will not want for a shelter while I have
four walls round me and a fire to warm my
hands.   And I would not wonder if she took
kindly to the ways of living here.   She'll
find a difference between Knockalanish and
Duntroone, in the living and the housing.

For well you know, Jess, it's not me that's
given to the over-praising of creature com-
forts; still, at the same time, I like what is
Christian; and I say that having cattle and
human beings under the same roof is not
Christian. It may be very healthy; but it
is not Christian. And never will I forget
the fortnight I spent at Knockalanish when
my sister was in her last illness; the damp
and the cold; the peats soaked through with
the snow; the supper of mashed potatoes
and milk; and the breathing of the cows in
the night. For of course my sister had the
ben * of the house; and the rest of us we
had to put up with what beds and screens
we could get; and night after night I was
lying awake, fearing to hear the tick of the
death-watch, or the howling of a dog, and it
was the breathing of the cows you could
hear, and not so far away. Ay. And
Donald Maclean he was never the good
manager, nor my poor sister either, but after
her death he lost heart altogether, and how
he was getting the rent, or whether there
was more and more of debt, no one could
tell; only this I am sure of, that when his
daughter Barbara comes to us, she will not

* The inner apartment.

bring with her anything more than what she stands up in——"

At this moment some one entered the shop, and Jess hurried away to attend. It was a clerkly-looking youth, who wanted a brier-root pipe; and very particular he was; but at length he was satisfied; whereupon Jess returned to the parlour.

"Then there's the lad Allan," continued the warm-hearted little widow, still busy with her knitting. "Well, now, I am glad that he sometimes looks in of an evening; and he is one the more to show to Barbara that she has come among her own kith and kin, though his mother married a Lowlander and he has partly a Lowland name. But this is it now, Jess, my lass, that when he stays to supper I wish you would be pressing a little more on him—yes, yes— I wish you would be pressing a little more on him——"

Jessie Maclean's fair face flushed somewhat.

"Allan Henderson is very proud, mother," she said. "And if he suspected anything he would never come back."

"Pride and an empty stomach," said the small dame, sententiously, "are not even

cousins twenty times removed. Starvation is
the worst of training for any one, I do not
care who he is ; and the young man is foolish
who refuses when there is plenty before him
on the table. But I have heard of Allan
and his ways; oh, yes, indeed : both his
father and his mother have told me; that
when he was at the College at Glasgow
he was costing them nothing—well, next to
nothing beyond the fees for the classes, and
the books, and a lodging; and now he is
paying back, and paying back, though they
are not asking for anything, and the post-
offus keeping them very comfortable now,
and I dare say he has paid them far more
than ever they lent him. Besides," she went
on, "it's a poor trade the schoolmastering.
It's very little the School Board give him,
after his hard work at the classes. And my
heart is sore to see a young man going about
at this time of the year without an overcoat
—when it's I myself would gladly buy him
one—and why should he not take it as a
present, from his mother's cousin—— "

The flush on the girl's face had deepened :
she turned to trim the fire by way of hiding
her vexation.

"You could not do that, mother !" she

exclaimed, in a low voice. " You would not insult him ?—and turn him away from the house ?—when he has not too many friends. And as for schoolmastering," she continued, raising her head—and at times speaking with an involuntary tremor of pride in her tones, " he may not be always a schoolmaster, though there are many schoolmasters that are great and famous men, at the large schools throughout the country. But if Allan is only a poor schoolmaster at present, it will not be always so, you may take my word for that. Of course he has not told me his plans and his hopes—why should he ?—I think he is too shy to tell them to anyone ; but I can see what he is ; I can see what there is in him ; and I know this, mother, that many a long day hence, you and I will be wondering that the Allan Henderson they are all talking of in London used to come into our parlour in Duntroone and smoke his pipe of an evening. It may be a long time yet ; but it will be a great day for us—even if he has no recollection of us ; and you'll bear me out, mother, that I prophesied it—— " Some slight noise arrested her attention, and she looked up. " Mercy on us, here's Allan himself ! " she ejaculated, in an undertone ; and therewith she rose to open the door for him—the colour not yet quite gone from her face.

He was a tall young man of about three or four-and-twenty, his figure slim and spare but well-knit, his head bent forward slightly, his features distinctly ascetic, yet with plenty of firmness about the lines of his mouth, his forehead square and capable, and showing a premature line or two, no doubt the result of hard and perhaps injudicious study. But it was his eyes that chiefly claimed attention : large, soft, brown eyes, that were usually contemplative and absent, but that could become singularly penetrating when his attention was challenged. It was a concentration, in obedience to any such summons, that appeared to demand some brief effort ; but his perceptions, once aroused, were swift ; he seemed instantly to divine whether this person or this utterance was worth heeding or to be turned away from with indifference and contempt. Jess used laughingly to say of him, when she was grown spiteful—

"Poor Allan, the matter with him is that there's a cloud betwixt him and all the world around him ; and when you think he is looking over to Lismore, or to Morven, or Kingairloch, it's the cloud he's staring at, and

the grand things he sees there—Roman
battles, and such like, I suppose.   And some
day he will be staring at the fine things
before him, and he'll step over the end of
the quay, and that will be the last of poor
Allan!"   And she would continue her flout-
ing: "Going on for four-and-twenty, and
as big a baby as ever he was in his childhood!
He has not got accustomed to anything!
Everything is new to him—and everything
wonderful—if he comes on a fox-glove growing in the woods—or watches a young foal
following its mother—or he'll pick up a shell
from the shore, and that's quite enough to
stare at and wonder at too!   And what he
gets to laugh at, passes me!—he'll burst out
laughing when there was no amusement
intended at all, and that is not pleasant to
people's feelings; or again, when the young
folk are a little merry, and mocking at each
other, he will sit as glum as if he was looking
at his own funeral going by.   Temper?—
temper, indeed!—he is the worst-tempered
young man in Duntroone!"

Yet the visitor who now came in did not
look as if he had an evil temper; rather he
seemed diffident as he took the seat that the
widow cheerfully offered him.

" I was passing," said he, by way of apology,
" and I thought I would step in to ask if you
had heard of your niece. Do you know if
the *Sanda* was able to call at Kilree?—the
weather has been bad out there."

" Well, it's little I am likely to hear,"
responded the widow, " until Barbara and
Lauchlan MacIntyre walk straight into the
shop, or come knocking at the door of the
house; though maybe some one will run up
from the quay to tell us when the *Sanda*
shows round the point. There's Tobermory,
to be sure, and they might have telegraphed
from Tobermory; but dear me, what does
that poor lass understand about the telegraph?
and Lauchlan—well, Lauchlan would be
amongst his friends. And yet I was caution-
ing him too. ' Lauchie,' I was saying to him,
' this time at least it is absolutely compara-
tive that you keep a hold on yourself, and
behave yourself at the funeral, and in bringing away the lass.' And he was saying ' Yes,
yes, mistress,' again and again. But I have
had experience of Lauchie, that is a good
enough man and a sensible man until the
whiskey gets over him; and when he begins
laughing, then it's a sign you need not try
to talk any more to him; and afterwards,

when he comes out of it and is sober again,
oh, the poor, down-hearted crayture that he
is !—as if he had committed every sin in the
Catalogue—— "

" You mean the Decalogue, mother ! " Jess
remonstrated.

" Ay : sometimes they say the one and
sometimes the other," the widow went on,
with blithe effrontery. " But I'm thinking
the *Sanda* should be in ere long now ; and
there's a bit supper waiting over the way ;
and it would be very agreeable to us, Allan,
if you would step across with us, when the
shop is shut, and take your place at the table,
to show Barbara that she has come amongst
several friends—— "

But he seemed to shrink back from this
proposal.

" No, no, thanks to you all the same," he
said—and he had a grave, gentle, impressive
voice, that Jess listened to as if every word
were of value. " When a girl comes to a
new home in this way, surely she would
rather be with her own people, and have no
half-strangers to meet. Afterwards there
will be plenty of time for her to make
acquaintances."

" And it is very ill done of you, Allan

Henderson," said the little widow, boldly and indignantly, "to speak of yourself as a stranger, or half-stranger, in my house. Perhaps these are the ways they have at the College; but I am not understanding such ways. Jess, she must be for ever making excuses; and it's this one's pride, and that one's pride; but I am not understanding such pride when there is the family-relationship between us. Oh, yes, every one has heard of the old saying about the Macleans and their pride and their poverty; ' Though I am poor, I am well-born; God be thanked I am a Maclean!' But where is the place for such things between cousins? And when you know very well, Allan, that over the way, and every night in the week, there is a place at the table for you, and Jessie and me sitting by ourselves, and perhaps you alone in your lodgings, and maybe without a fire, too—for I have heard of such things with young men eager to get on in the world—well, then, it may be.College manners for you to stay away, but it is not good Highland manners. And that is the truth I am telling you at last."

Jess Maclean looked apprehensive and troubled; but the young man took all this in good part.

" One is not always one's own master," he
answered, quietly. " I can only give you
my best thanks for so kindly asking me.
And I am sure you know another old saying :
' If a man cannot get to his own country, it
is a good thing to be in sight of it ' ? "

" Will you not light your pipe now,
Allan ? " Jess put in skilfully—to get away
from a ticklish subject.

But at this suggestion, Mrs. Maclean, who
had been regarding the young man (perhaps
with some little compunction, for she was
not accustomed to scold) quickly rose from
her seat and left the room, disappearing into
the front shop, and evidently bent on some
errand.

" I hope you are not vexed with my mother,
Allan," said Jess, at once.

" Oh, no, indeed," he made answer. " Every
one knows that she is the kindest of women.
And when your cousin comes from the
islands, she will soon find that she is in a
friendly home."

Presently Mrs. Maclean reappeared, bringing with her an unopened tin canister.

" This is a new mixture, Allan," said she,
as she placed the box before the young man,
" that has been sent me from Glasgow, and

I would be glad if you would take the canister home with you, and try the mixture, and tell me your opinion, so that I could be advising my customers when they come in. Will you put it in your pocket, or will I send Christina along with it to you in the morning?"

Jess looked swiftly and in alarm from one to the other of them. But if his stubborn Scotch independence prompted him to refuse the gift, the Highland blood that also flowed in his veins forbade that the refusal should be in any way discourteous. He hesitated for a second—to find some excuse; and there was some colour of embarrassment visible on his forehead.

"I am very much obliged to you, Mrs. Maclean," said he, after this involuntary pause. "But—but I have been thinking of giving up my pipe altogether."

And now the anxiety of the younger woman gave place to an infinite distress and pity: was he—simply because he had been driven into a corner, and found himself unable to refuse in any other manner this proffered kindness—was he going to deprive himself of the chief, perhaps the only, comfort of a poor and solitary student?

But at this moment her attention was

distracted. Some one entered the shop, and approached the dividing door; and a glance through the half-curtained pane told her who this was—this was Mr. Peter McFadyen, coal merchant and town-councillor. She rose to receive the new visitor: but she did so with impatient anger in her heart: for she knew that now in a very few minutes the proud and contemptuous Allan would be on his homeward way.

CHAPTER III.

YET Peter McFadyen himself was about the
last man in the world to imagine that he
could be unwelcome anywhere; and as he
now, after salutations and inquiries, proceeded to make himself comfortable in front
of the fire—pulling out his pipe and tobacco-
pouch the while—he went on to give these
neighbours a vivid account of his day's
doings on the golf-links, nothing doubting
of their sympathy and keen interest. He
was a little man, round and chubby, with
eager, twinkling eyes, a clipped sandy-brown
beard, and hair becoming conspicuously scant
on the top. For the rest, the rumour in
Duntroone was that McFadyen, who was
an old bachelor, had it in view to amalga-
mate his fortunes with those of the widow;

but some there were who surmised that
Peter cherished other and more romantic
designs.

"Dod," he said, with a triumphant chuckle,
"I'm thinking the station-master and me
we were showing the young fellows something this afternoon! Not that I would
call either Mr. Gilmour or myself elderly
folk—— "

"Indeed, Mr. McFadyen," said the widow,
politely, "it will be many a long day before
you can think of such a thing."

"A few years one way or the other is
nothing at all," responded Mr. McFadyen,
with obvious satisfaction. "Just nothing
at all! It is a question of keeping yourself
in good fettle; and if one of they young
fellows and myself were to start away from
Taynuilt, I wonder which of us would be
the first to reach the top of Cruachan Ben.
Ay, or throwing the hammer: that is a
capital test of what is in a man's shoulders;
and I should not be afraid of a match with
some of them—not me! I've got a practis-
ing-place marked out in the backyard—
though it's rather narrow—and if anybody
was a bit careless, the hammer would make
a fearfu' smash of the little greenhouse—— "

" Did I ever thank you for the christmas-anthemums, Mr. McFadyen?" the widow interposed. "They were just beautiful—though Jessie was sorry you should be cutting them——"

But Peter was not to be diverted from vaunting his physical prowess.

"Running—jumping—pulling an oar," he continued, with buoyant assurance (and perhaps widening out his chest a little, for he must have known that Jessie Maclean's ' grey eyes feminine' were now regarding him) "give me a week or two's training, and I'm not afraid of any of they boasting young chaps. But it's the links, Mrs. Maclean, it's the links I was coming to ; and we did well there this afternoon, I can tell you! We did well, both Gilmour and me ; but I beat him—the fact is, Gilmour is a little thing stiff in the joints, though he doesna like to hear it said. Well, we started from the teeing-ground just behind the Dunchoillie farm ; and you know Colquhoun's meadow, Mrs. Maclean, there's a burn comes down through the middle, and then there's a bank covered with whin-bushes : it's just a desperate bunker to get into. Very well : I put the ball on the tee—a little sand; not too much sand; too much sand's a great mistake—and I let drive! Dod, that was a drive! Away she went with a ping like a rifle-bullet—sailing and sailing—sailing and sailing—and getting smaller and smaller—until my eyes were filled wi' water staring against the white clouds—and Gilmour he lost sight of the ball altogether. 'It's down in the whins!' he cries. 'Ye gomeril,' I answers him, 'it's more near the putting-green, if not close up to the hole!'— for I was just certain I had got far away over the burn and the whins, and was safe on to the higher land. Would you believe it?—when we got up, the ball was within twenty yards of the flag; and in three more strokes I was out; the first hole for four!— and me that never touched a golf-club until last summer!"

Peter had been growing excited: he now moderated his warmth.

"I did not do so well at the second hole," he observed darkly. "Maybe it was the wind; or maybe I toed the ball when I was driving from the tee; anyway it got over the dyke and into the road, ay, and into the cart-rut, and I thought I was never going to get it over the dyke again. Bother the thing, I smashed my iron niblick clean in two—but—but I'm thinking there must have been a flaw in the wood—— "

He hastened away from these deplorable reminiscences.

" The Pinnacle!" he said, laughing with eager anticipation. " We had a rare game at the Pinnacle! For that's a most desperate place, Mrs. Maclean, and no mistake—as steep as the side of a house—and all soomin with water—and unless you get clear away on to the top, what happens is that your ball strikes the face of the hill, and doesna lie there, but just comes quietly trintle, trintle, trintling down the slope and back to your feet again. And there was I up on the top —right up on the putting-green, after a fine long drive—looking down on Gilmour; and I declare there never was such an angry man !— hacking away with his cleek—splashing the mud—and sweerin' every time the ball would come trintle, trintling back down to his feet. ' Gilmour,' I cries to him, ' put the ball in your pocket, man, and bring it up with ye : it's the only way at the Pinnacle !' And he would not speak, so angry he was; and still angrier was he when we started away for the next hole; for he forgot it was blowing up

there on the top—blowing right across from
Mull and Morven and the Frith of Lorn;
and he put far too much sand on the tee—
far too much sand, for he's an obstinate man,
Gilmour, and will not take a telling—and in
his anger he made a drive that should have
sent the ball over to Lismore! Did it?"
Peter asked—and he roared with laughter,
and his small eyes twinkled, and he rubbed
his hands. "There was just a blash of sand!
—a blash of sand—that rose in the air—
and back it came in his face—just filling
his eyes, and filling his mouth, so that he
went about splutterin', and could not even
sweer! Dod, the station-master was an
angry man this afternoon!—it's a fearfu'
place the Pinnacle!"

At this point the tall and grave young
schoolmaster rose to go, notwithstanding a
half-concealed deprecatory glance from Jess.

"Allan, my lad," said Mr. McFadyen,
familiarly, "have you heard of the dance
that Mr. and Mrs. McAskill of the Argyll
Arms are going to give to the Gaelic
Choir?"

"No," said the schoolmaster, somewhat
curtly.

"Yes, indeed, then," continued Peter, with

much importance. "In the Volunteer Drill-
Hall. A great affair, for the Choir will sing
glees between the dances, and there'll be
plenty of pipers. And sure I am that every
one in this room at this minute will have
an invite; and I have been thinking, Mrs.
Maclean, that if you would let me call for
you and Miss Jessie, I would bring a machine
and drive you up to the Drill-Hall, for it's a
bad road in the dark, and it would never do
for you and Miss Jessie to get your feet
wet——"

"Mr. McFadyen," said Jess, with some
touch of resentment, "I think you are
forgetting what has just happened in our
family——"

"Oh, but the dance is a long way off yet!"
said Peter. And then he went on, with
humorous shyness: "Maybe, if any one
should have a doubt about going, maybe
that one's myself: maybe they'll be saying
that my dancing days should be over——"

"And who could be saying that!" interposed the widow, promptly. "That would
be nonsense indeed! I should not wonder,
now, if you could give lessons to some of
those young lads and lasses."

He turned to her with sudden seriousness.

"If there's one thing surer than another, Mrs. Maclean," he said, "it's this—that a well-trained step is never forgotten. Begin well—that's everything in dancing; and ye acquire a grace—an elegance, I might say— that becomes a kind of second nature. Not that I object to a rough-and-tumble reel now and again; no, no; I'm not more afraid of a foursome reel than I am of a foursome round on the links. But there's something finer.— Miss Jessie, do you know the Varsoviana?"

"I have seen it," Jess Maclean answered, coldly.

"But it's the simplest thing—the simplest thing in the world!" he vehemently urged. "Just stand up for a minute, now, and I'll show ye——"

He himself got up, put his toes into the first position, and held out his hand to encourage her. But she declined to move.

"If you please, I would rather not, Mr. McFadyen," she said, with flushed face.

"But look!" said he. And therewith, whistling an air with pursed lips, he proceeded to execute certain short, stiff, marionette-like movements, as well as he could in the circumscribed space at his disposal.

"D'you see now?—as simple as simple!—

then lead off with the next foot—the other
foot at every turn—d'ye see how simple it
is?—and the most elegant thing that ever
was seen, with a lot of couples in a ball-
room." He ceased from these valorous efforts,
and resumed his chair, proud, breathless, and
happy. "We'll get you to have a try at
it some other evening, Miss Jessie," said he,
gaily. "I'm thinking we'll be able to show
them something the night of Mrs. McAskill's
dance!"

Allan Henderson had been waiting
patiently, not wishing to interrupt.

"I will bid you good-evening now, Mrs.
Maclean," said he.

"Good-night, Allan," she made answer,
holding out her hand.

But Jess followed him into the front shop,
shutting the door behind her.

"I am sorry if Mr. McFadyen and his
blethers have driven you away, Allan: you do
not come to see us as much as you might."

"I must get home to my books," he
answered her, evasively.

"And I hope, Allan," she said, regarding
him with anxious and earnest eyes, "that you
are not working too hard at your studies."

"Well," said he, "when one is young one

must work hard. It is the only time : there
is no after time. But I'll be looking in to
see you and your mother again one of these
evenings. Good-night, Jessie."

"Good-night, Allan !" said she ; and when
he had gone, she lingered a while : she did
not care to return at once to the parlour,
where doubtless Mr. McFadyen was still
engaged in magnifying his strength, his
agility, and innumerable accomplishments.

On the other hand, Allan, when he left the
tobacconist's shop, did not immediately return
to his lodging and his books. He was at an
age, and in circumstances, that imperatively
demanded close and strenuous self-communion;
and that he was accustomed to seek in solitary
walks along the seashore, or up on the
moorland wastes, especially at night, when
darkness and silence were abroad. And
tumultuous indeed were the problems he
found confronting him in these lonely
rambles. There were deep and inscrutable
searchings of heart, for no matter what his
training and his traditions may have been,
he was resolute and uncompromising in his
search after such truth as might be discover-
able—about human nature, and the surroundings of human nature, and the more awful

mysteries beyond; there were ambitious
projects springing thick from an over-active
brain—elusive, distracting phantoms that just
as often as not beat wild wings against the
res angusta domi; the *res angusta domi* itself
came in with its sordid cares and pinchings—
the need of a pair of weather-proof boots—
the counting the cost of a holiday-trip to see
his father and mother, who kept the post-
office at Inverblair—this latest project of
giving up tobacco—and the like; while
ever-recurrent were the vague and harassing
visions of youth—that troubled questioning
of the future, with all its tantalising hopes,
its looming anxieties, its hidden dangers and
pitfalls. But happily for him, in this
seething-time, in this time of storm and
stress, he had been spared the crowning
misery of all. The 'cruel madness of love'
had not overtaken him : that honeyed poison-
cup at all events had not been placed to
his lips.

He passed through the now half-dormant
town, went round the obscure and silent
quays, ascended a steep incline, and eventually, emerging from the black shadow of
some larches, stepped out upon a little plateau
on the summit of the Gallows Hill. It was

a favourite resort of his : here he could pace
up and down, exorcising the demons of
unrest and doubt and despondency, and
bidding the great surrounding mountains
lend some little measure of their invulnerable
calm.   On this particular night, it is true,
the darkness was such that nothing was
visible of all those vast mountain-ranges ;
but well he knew the whereabouts of the
mighty peaks and shoulders, from Ben Buie
and Creachbeinn and Dun-da-gu, over in
Mull, to Glashven and Fuar Bheinn up in
Morven, from the far giants of Glencoe,
murmuring to each other across the silence
of the valleys, round to Ben Cruachan and
Ben Eunaich, above the lonely and ghostly
solitudes of Glen-strae.   August companions,
to be sure, even if unseen ; they appeared
to lift the soul away from the trivial tasks
and frettings of everyday life ; these he
seemed for the moment to have left behind
him—down in yonder little town, that he
could now make out only by certain glow-
worm dots scattered here and there, indi-
cating the semicircular sweep of the bay.

Of a sudden his eyes were attracted else-
whither.   Far away at the back of Kerrara
island a white shaft of fire had sprung into

the mirk of the night—a distant, trembling, curving, silent thing that glared for a second or so, and then vanished, leaving the darkness as impenetrable as before. And for a moment he asked himself whether the Mull people—the people down about Duart—were setting off fireworks. But what occasion could there be for fireworks? The next instant another slender white shaft rose silent into the air; and now, judging by the position of the Lismore light—the one steady, radiant star in all this wide, black picture— these signals seemed to be coming from some point between Lismore and Mull. But signals?—not fireworks at all? And if signals, then signals from some vessels in distress? And what vessel was now expected, except the *Sanda*, that was bringing to the household of the Macleans the young girl from the outer isles?

He sped away down the hill-side and gained the dusky thoroughfares. The few people about had not noticed the signals—perhaps the northern end of Kerrara island had prevented their being seen. But soon there was sufficient commotion in the little town; and one old sailor, hurrying along with his companions to a commanding point, to discover what had happened or was happening, was heard to say to himself—

"The *Sanda?* But the *Sanda* would be coming over from Craigenure? And how the duffle could she get so far down to the west?"

CHAPTER IV.

ON A ROCK.

Now when the *Sanda* left Craigenure, Long
Lauchlan the shoemaker was down in the
fore-cabin, snugly huddled up in a corner;
and he was nursing a soda-water bottle half-
filled with whiskey, while he softly sang to
himself. It was not a lugubrious song; but
lugubriously and slowly he sang it, especially
the refrain—

> ' *If ye'll walk,*
> *If ye'll walk,*
> *If ye'll walk with me anywhere* '

the *a*'s in which he pronounced as the *a* in
dark, dwelling on them indefinitely. Red
Murdoch the Mull drover, who had been
having a royal time of it since these two
left Kilree, and who chanced to be the only
other occupant of the cabin, at length interrupted angrily.

"To the devil with your south-country songs!" he cried, in Gaelic.

But the long, melancholy-visaged shoe-maker took no offence; he was too happy.

"It's a beautiful song—a beautiful song," he said, also in Gaelic. "And if it is a south-country song, it is a song that is known to every fisherman from Peterhead to Buckie. There is no more favourite song." He raised his forefinger, to beat the slow time. "A beautiful song—

> ' It's I will buy you a pennyworth of preens,
>   If ye'll walk,
>   If ye'll walk,
>   If ye'll walk with me anywhere.' "

"The man is a fool that would sing such a song!" said the red-bearded drover, bluntly.

Whereupon Lauchie laughed and chuckled quietly to himself.

"Oh, yes, I may be a fool. But I would rather be a fool than a man with bad luck."

"Who is a man with bad luck?" demanded Murdoch, his bushy eyebrows drawing together.

Lauchie appeared to be secretly amused.

"Then you do not know you are of the same name with the man of bad luck?" he went on. "Oh, you do not know what they

say of the luck of Red Murdoch? They say
to any one 'You have the luck of Red
Murdoch; for when Red Murdoch is in the
north, then the herring are in the south.'"

"If I knew the man that said that of me,"
rejoined Murdoch, with fiery eyes—and he
even thrust forth a massive and hairy fist,
clenched, to give emphasis to his threat, " I
would bash his head against a stone wall."

"Have a dram, Murdoch," said Lauchie,
tendering the bottle, which was not refused.
"It's not I that am going out of the house
to-night, no, not to fight anyone. I am a
peaceable person. Better a warm fireside
than a cold hill-side, that is what the wise
man of Ross was saying. Murdoch," he
continued, suddenly reverting to the blissful
days that were now nearing an end, "it was
a beautiful funeral. That is what I am
thinking. It was a beautiful funeral. There
was no parsimony. How many gallons of
whiskey, would you say?—seven?—ay, ay,
and maybe more like seven and a half.
There was two or three glasses apiece when
we came together; and there was two more
at the house; well, that was right and
proper; and although it is not easy for
eight men to keep in step, when they have

a heavy coffin on their shoulders, there was
not a single man fell into the road, and each
time the coffin was set down, it was set down
as gently as if it were a cradle, not a coffin
at all. And two more glasses to each man
at the gate of the cemetery. And two more
coming away. After that—aw, God, I am
not remembering much—there was little use
in counting—— but sure I am there was no
parsimony; and it was the fine funeral that
was given to Donald Maclean of Knockalanish. Have you a match, Murdoch?"

"I am tired of giving matches to a fool of
a man that will not carry them for himself,"
answered Red Murdoch, sulkily and taunt-
ingly.

But Lauchie would not quarrel. He re-
signedly put his pipe in his pocket again; he
settled himself in a corner, his head drooping
somewhat; and he resumed his placid and
happy communing with himself.

"A beautiful song—not a fisherman from
Peterhead to Buckie but knows it—a beautiful
song—

' *It's I will buy you a braw new gown,*
With buttons so fine, and flounces to the ground,
If ye'll waak,
If ye'll waak,
If ye'll waak with me anywhere.'

A beautiful song. . . . And a beautiful
funeral . . . no parsimony at all——"

Then his head fell wholly: he was fast
asleep. Red Murdoch glanced at him with
angry scorn; threw a parting oath at him;
and turned to leave the cabin. And this
he managed, after several efforts—for the
steps of the companion were narrow and
exceedingly steep—to do: hands, knees, and
feet were all brought into requisition; and
eventually he emerged into the upper air.

Meanwhile what had become of the young
lass from the outer isles whom these two
worthies were convoying to Duntroone?
Once or twice she had been invited to go
down into the fore-cabin; but she had
refused—for the odour of the place was
overpowering; she preferred to remain on
deck; and the steward had considerately
brought her some tea and some food. She
had got into a more or less sheltered place
well away forward; and there she sate with
her tartan shawl drawn close around her,
silent and solitary, and half-terrified by the
strange things around her. For she had
never been on a steamer before; and although
the monotony of the long voyage had produced a state of semi-stupefaction, she

remained nervously alive to all her surroundings—to the throbbing of the screw, the lash of the waves along the vessel's side, and the dusky figures moving about the deck. The night was obscure and squally; but at least there was no rain; and the high bulwarks were a sort of protection to her against the hurling gusts of wind.

Now there had come on board at Craigenure two gentlemen who were returning home to Duntroone—one of them, indeed, the principal doctor there, the other a well-known bailie; and these two had wandered up to the bow of the ship to look around them; and they were chatting to each other. Barbara Maclean heard every word.

"Surely we're keeping a long way from Lismore, Bailie," the Doctor said, regarding the steady and golden ray of the lighthouse that was shining boldly through the mirk of the night. "I wonder how many times I have crossed from Craigenure and yet I never saw a course like this taken before."

"Maybe Pattison is trying to cheat the tide," replied the Bailie. "There's fearful tides running here at times."

"Well, Captain Pattison should know his own business best," the Doctor was saying—

when of a sudden he gripped his companion's
arm. "What's that there—right ahead!"
he exclaimed, staring with amazement and
consternation at some vague, half-invisible,
dark object that seemed to loom up out of
the water. And then again, instantly recognising what was about to happen, he called
out—"It's the Lady Rock! For God's sake,
man, hold on!—hold on to something!"—
while he himself caught at the nearest
portion of the standing rigging, and braced
himself as best he might to withstand the
coming crash.

There appeared to be no interval. Almost
simultaneously with his shouted warning
came the inevitable, the terrific shock that
seemed to rive the ship from stem to stern;
then she lurched forward and upward, with
a hideous grinding sound; then she dipped
somewhat; and then she hung—hung there
for one dreadful second of silence, as if she
were some dumb animal mutely asking what
was next required of her—whether she
should carry on some half-dozen yards
farther, and, with smashed bows and started
plates, go headlong to the bottom, in fifty
fathoms of water. But no: she remained
firm: and she remained upright, though

with a strong list to starboard; and now, after that one moment of paralysed silence and suspense, an indescribable clamour and commotion ensued—women shrieking and running hither and thither for their relatives, the sailors hurrying along with lanterns, the captain calling his orders from the bridge. And all through this bewilderment of noise and confusion there ran the ominous hoarse surge of the tide on the isolated rocks beneath and around them; it was as a voice out of the unseen; and it was a clamorous and an angry voice—a voice that threatened doom.

Barbara Maclean had been thrown violently on to the deck; but when she raised herself, she had no thought of rushing about, claiming protection and succour. Her faculties had been stunned and blunted by these terrors of the sea and of the night; and when she resumed her place, she only pulled her shawl around her, cowering, and perhaps crying a little in her helplessness. She knew nothing of what was going forward. She saw dark figures going quickly about with lanterns; but they did not chance to come near her; and even in that case she would have been too timid to put any

question. It is true, she did utter a brief cry
of dismay when the first rocket, with a shrill
and sudden scream, sprung high and blinding into the gloom; but in time she got used
even to that; while the intermittent thunder
of the signal-cannon only seemed to shake
her frame physically. She was too dazed
to feel further or acute alarm; what might
happen would have to happen; she was far
away from her own land, and from things
with which she was familiar. As for the two
men who had in a kind of fashion undertaken
to see her safely to Duntroone, neither was
of near relationship to her, and she could not
expect much care from them; besides she
knew the ways of people who had been
to a Highland funeral out in the west; and
she was content to remain unassisted and
alone.

The odd thing was that in such a crisis of
danger Red Murdoch should have thought
first, not of this forlorn creature, but of his
boon companion, with whom he was con-
stantly quarrelling. He stumbled along to
the fore-cabin; he steadied himself at the top
of the companion; he howled aloud his
warning; and then, finding there was no
reply, he made his way—to speak plainly, he

fell—down the steps; he crossed the floor, and seized Lauchie MacIntyre by the coat-collar.

"Here, man, come away!—do you not understand?—we may all of us be at the bottom of the sea in a minute!—"

Lauchie endeavoured, but in a gentle manner, to repel this interference.

"No," he said, slowly, but firmly, "I will not stir from the house this night. It is I that am knowing when I am well off. Go away yourself, Murdoch. It's a warm house I am in; and a warm house is better than a cold hill-side——"

"Son of the Devil!" roared Murdoch, furiously. "Do you not know that we are on a rock?"

"And the house that is founded on a rock is a beautiful house," said Lauchie, solemnly. "Have you a match, Murdoch?"

Murdoch did not answer, but now with both hands he seized the coat-collar of the shoemaker, and by main force dragged him to the foot of the companion. Then first he tried to shove him up the steps; next he tried to drag him up; presently they both fell together; and it is impossible to say what might have happened had not a sailor, hearing some noise, come to the top of the companion, and called down—

" Uss there any one below there? "

" Yes, indeed," called Murdoch in reply. " Come here and give me a little assustance with a friend of mine, that uss rather too sleepy to go ashore by himself."

The sailor came running down the companion; and fortunately he was a powerfully built man.

" Going ashore? " said he, grimly, as he proceeded to hoist and shoulder these two up the steps. " It's miles aweh from any shore you are! And the sooner you are out of this boat the better: would you like to be left behind? "

For now it appeared that the captain had decided that the passengers, at least, should descend from the steamer, taking such precarious chance of safety as might be afforded by the solitary reef on which they had struck. The gangway was open; a ladder affixed; and by the dusky glare of two lamps woman after woman, and man after man, went down the side, to seek out for some footing among the wet and slippery seaweed and the hidden pools of salt water. They crowded together, these poor wretches, deafened by the rush and roar of the tides all around them ; and perhaps wondering when those baleful forces would arise out of the dark and seize and engulf them. They dared hardly move, for a single false step might plunge them into unknown deeps; and the lights of the steamer were dim. Those indeed were best off who could cling on to the massive iron bars of the beacon that marks the rock—a flameless skeleton of a structure that towered away above them into the sombre skies. And meanwhile, at intervals, from the deck of the ship, the rockets went screaming into the night, and the signal cannon boomed its reverberations across the waste of waves. But half-hour after half-hour went by, and there was no response.

"They can neither see nor hear us," the Doctor said to his neighbour. "We are too far away for the sound to carry. And Kerrara lies between us and Duntroone : they will not see the rockets."

"But surely the people at Lismore light must see them !" said the Bailie.

"Yes, indeed, that is possible. But they have no telegraph there."

"No telegraph at the lighthouse?" exclaimed the Bailie, indignantly. "Then it is a monstrous and mischievous shame! A fine piece of economy! Who is responsible for that—the Board of Trade?" And then he added: "But at least they have a boat at the lighthouse?"

"Ay, but not a boat that would be of much use to us, across that driving sea."

Nevertheless the captain was about to tempt those stormy waters, in hopes of obtaining assistance from the mainland. In the dull glow of the lamps, the shipwrecked crowd could perceive the boat being lowered from the side of the stranded vessel; presently the mate and two of the hands had got into it; and in a few minutes it had disappeared—into the mysterious surrounding chaos. There was no cheer raised as the boat departed; this small assemblage of folk, hardly visible to each other, and hardly to be distinguished from the blackness of the reef, was too dispirited and perturbed; Duntroone and the possibilities of help were miles away; while the dangers immediately encompassing them were pressing and near.

"When the tide rises, how many of us could clamber up and hold on to the beacon?" asked the Bailie of his companion.

Barbara Maclean heard this question put,

but did not divine its import. She was standing alone and friendless and helpless; weeping silently; her shawl not much of a protection now against the blasts of wind tearing across the exposed reef. She was benumbed with cold and misery; not knowing what might happen: conscious, too, that all her little possessions — her chest, containing everything she owned in the world —had been left on board the steamer—the steamer that at any moment might slip forward and vanish from before their eyes, into fifty fathoms of ocean.

CHAPTER V.

THE *FIREFLY*.

WHEN the young schoolmaster, alarmed by those signals of distress that rose white and silent into the distant night, sped away down from the Gallows Hill, he made straight for the house of the agent of the Steam Packet Company.

"It may be the *Sanda*," said the agent, at once hurrying off to get his overcoat and hat. "She's hours late as it is. Anyway we must run out to see what is the matter; and luckily the *Firefly* lighter is lying at the quay : she'll not be long in getting up steam."

"Would you let me go with you, Mr. Stewart ?" Allan asked.

"Why not ? Why not ? You're the first to bring the news——"

" For there's a young lass," Allan ex-
plained, " coming by the *Sanda* from Kilree :
she's a niece of Mrs. Maclean in Campbell
Street; and the Macleans would take it as a
friendly thing if I went out to see if there
was anything to be done for her—— "

" Why not ? " said the good-natured agent;
and he took up his stick, which was his
symbol of authority, and opened the door for
himself and his companion.

" And would there be time for me to run
round to Mrs. Maclean's and get a few wraps
and things of that kind ? " continued Allan.
" The night is cold."

" Well, yes, if you are quick about it; but
you must not keep me waiting," said the
agent, as he hastened away on his own
errand, along the dark and wet sea-front.

It took the tall young schoolmaster but
a minute or two to reach Mrs. Maclean's
house—the shop being now shut.

" And is the *Sanda* coming in at last ? "
cried the cheerful little widow. " And will
there be time for Jessie and me to go down
to meet Barbara ? "

" Well, no," said Allan, with a trifle of
hesitation. " The *Sanda* is not in sight yet.
But there's a ship out there in some kind of

trouble; and I'm going out with Mr. Stewart, in a lighter; and I was thinking—if it was the *Sanda*—well, I might take a few things that might be of use to your niece, for the weather has been very wet and rough lately—"

At the mere suggestion that anything had happened, or might be happening, to the steamer bringing her niece Barbara to Duntroone, the widow became quite unnerved with fright; and her anxious and irrelevant questions, to which there was no possible answer, were nothing but a stumbling-block in the way. It was Jess who was the helpful one—who instantly divined what was wanted. In the briefest space of time she had cleverly put together a serviceable bundle of shawls and wraps, to say nothing of a pair of mittens, a paper bag of sweet biscuits, and a flask of some innocent cordial. And with these things he was speeding away—indeed, he had got well down the staircase—when at the last moment Jess called to him again.

" Allan!—Allan !"

He looked up. She came running down the stone steps (for the Macleans lived in a small tenement of flats) and by the uncertain light he saw that she held something in her hand.

"If you are going out in the steamer," said she, " will you not put this muffler round your neck ? It may be a coarse night outside the bay."

Well, he was loth to offend this gentle half-cousin of his ; but still—still—there was something in the man's nature that drove him to refuse.

" No, thank you, Jessie," he said. " No, thank you—I am not afraid of the cold."

" Oh," said she, " if you will not take it because you think it is one of the things that women wear, then that is not very friendly. If I were you, I would not be so proud !"

The light in the stairway was dim ; it was the tone of her voice that told him he had vexed her.

" Oh, then, I will take it," he said, " and maybe it will be of use to your cousin Barbara." And therewith he hurried off again, for he was anxious not to keep Mr. Stewart waiting.

As he passed along, it became apparent that the news had spread through the little town of something having happened to the *Sanda*—or perhaps some other vessel—outside ; and when he reached the quay, there

was quite a group of folk, mostly superan-
nuated fishermen, eagerly discussing the possibilities. The steam-lighter was ready to
start; as soon as he got on board, the ropes
were thrown off, the blades of the screw
began to lash the water, and the high-bowed,
unwieldy craft was soon moving crescent-
wise out into the bay. And then, as she
gathered speed, the dull orange points that
told of the window-panes of Duntroone—
along the shore and up on the hill-side—
gradually receded; and ahead of them was
a great black world of invisible mountain
and sea and sky, with ever and always the
solitary ray of Lismore lighthouse burning
steadfast and clear.

" If the *Sanda's* engines have broken down
over there," said Mr. Stewart, " the mouth
of the Sound of Mull is a bad place. There
will be a strong ebb tide running, and she
may drift just anywhere."

" But the rockets I saw," Allan made
answer, " seemed all to rise from the same
spot; and as far as I could make out, that
would be over near the Lady Rock, or somewhere in that direction."

" If Pattison has got the *Sanda* on to the
Lady Rock," observed the agent, " the sooner

he sends in his certificate to the Board of Trade the better. But it's not believable !— he's an experienced man——"

The remarkable thing, however, was that though they had by this time rounded Kerrara point, there was no sign of any vessel anywhere—no repetition of those swift white messengers that had attracted Allan Henderson's attention when he was on the top of the Gallows Hill. The night, it is true, was pitch-dark and squally, and there were occasional gusts of rain flying about; but all the same they were now out in the open, and a ship's rocket ought to have been visible a great distance off.

"Allan, lad," said Mr. Stewart, " I hope you have not brought us on a wild-goose-chase."

And Allan himself began to think back. His eyes could not have deceived him ? He had never been subject to hallucinations, even when he was working hardest at his studies—with scant fuel for the engine. And surely there could be no mistake about his actually having beheld those long shafts of silvery fire spring into the black heavens ?

" I think I wass seeing a light," called the man who was peering over the bows, "just about right ahead, and no so far aweh."

All eyes were now eagerly turned in one direction.

" Ay, there it is !—there it is ! " called one after the other—as an ineffectual glimmer flickered just above the waves, and then vanished.

"It's a small boat—most likely with a message," said Mr. Stewart to the owner of the lighter. " Slack down your speed, Thomson, and let them take their own time about coming near."

The next instant there was another brief flare among the unseen waves ahead, but only for an instant: the people in the rowing boat had presumably lit a bunch of paper, to warn the steamer of their whereabouts, and the wind had directly blown out the flame. Nevertheless they at last got within hailing distance—though with great caution, for the unwieldy lighter was rolling heavily.

" We're from the *Sanda,*" came a hoarse voice through the darkness.

" Who are you ? "

" The mate and two of the hands."

" Where is she ? "

" On the Lady Rock."

"Bless me, how did she get on to the Lady Rock?"

Silence.

"No harm to passengers or crew?"

"Not yet," was the evasive answer.

"Steamer damaged?"

"Ay. I'm thinking her back's brokken. The passengers are ahl out on the rock."

"Well, we'll go over and fetch them off."

"Is it Mr. Stewart?"

"Yes."

"Are we to go on to Duntroone?"

"No. We'll want your boat; and we'll want you too. Come on board; and we'll tow the boat astern."

It was a difficult business on so rough and dark a night; for the men in the smaller boat had a wholesome fear of the lurching and pitching of this great heavy brute of a thing; but at last they managed it; and the *Firefly* was sent on again, with such speed as she was capable of making. It turned out that the mate had no story to tell. How the *Sanda* had got on to the Lady Rock was all a mystery. Or perhaps he deemed it prudent, in the circumstances, to hold his peace.

Then in course of time they began to make out, through the mirk and the wet, certain

minute dots of light, dim and wavering in
the distance, and sometimes almost disappearing, as a thick squall of rain would drive
by. But when they drew nearer they perceived that certain of these tremulous points
of fire appeared to be stationary, while others
were moving like mysterious will-o'-the-wisps
over the black water; and they guessed that
the sailors, furnished with lanterns, were
perhaps making such small provision of comfort as was possible for the people huddled
together on the reef. And here were two
other lights, one red and one green : the port
and starboard lights of the stranded ship.

" Well, I'm sure ! " exclaimed Mr. Stewart.
" She's right on the top of the rock ! "

" Ay," said the mate, who was standing by
him, " she's well up and over. She's on this
side—and lying nearly due east and west."

" Was the man trying to steeplechase her ! "
the agent demanded—but the mate was discreetly deaf.

Meanwhile the speed of the steam-lighter
had been slowed down until she was doing
little more than holding her own against the
wind and the fierce-running tide—the owner
having no kind of wish to go nearer that
dangerous reef than he could help.

" We'll try the first landing with your boat," said Mr. Stewart to the mate. " Since you came away, you should know the road back. And do not take us too close under the bows of the *Sanda*, for she might slip forward even yet."

" If she slips forward a few yards," said the mate, " she'll go straight to the bottom."

" And will you go with us, Allan, lad ? " continued Mr. Stewart. " Or will you wait on board the lighter ? "

" Well, I would rather go with you," the schoolmaster said, " and take an oar. There'll be somebody wanted up at the bow anyway."

And so, after some delay, the boat was hauled alongside; and they jumped or scrambled into it, and got out the oars, and no doubt were glad enough to shove away from the immediate neighbourhood of the lumbering craft. As yet no figures were discernible on the black reef ahead of them ; but the dots of yellow light were there—and they were kept briskly moving : this was the last form of signalling left to the stranded folk, after the rockets had all been expended.

And now, even though they were creeping in under the lee, they could hear the appalling

roar of the surf all around these rocks ; and
they imagined that their coming would not
be unwelcome to the castaways. Apparently
for their better guidance, those golden glowworms that had been scattered about now
seemed to converge ; they appeared to be
coming close down to the water ; and yet
they were kept moving, as if to indicate
where some creek had been discovered ;
while the man at the bow of the boat, as she
got closer and closer, from time to time called
aft to his companions.

"No so hard, Hughie ! Back-watter,
man ! Back-watter, both of you ! No—you
pull a stroke, Mr. Henderson !"

" Ay, ay, in here—in here ! " shouted the
voices from the rock—and the glowworms
were clustered together now, shedding a dull
glare on the seaweed and the dark water and
on a small group of phantasmal figures.

Well, they were willing hands that were
laid on the gunwale of the boat, when the
swirl of an eddying wave lifted her near
enough to be caught ; and up she went on
the slippery seaweed, until she was found to
be secure ; then the rescuers stepped out,
and Allan got hold of his bundle. It was
the strangest sight that met his eyes. The

black reef; the massive black hull of the steamer—chiefly indicated by the obscure illumination still remaining in the ports of the saloon and fore-cabin; the black bars of the beacon, that rose away up into the pitchy skies; the black figures that stood about in detached groups, or stepped warily forward through the seaweed to hear what the new-comers proposed to do: all these were surrounded by a wavering, uncertain, half-impenetrable gloom, for the air was thick with spray and rain, and the wind was blowing hard. Presently, however, one or two of the lamps were brought along, and the sombre phantoms began to take more recognisable shape. Here, for example, was Long Lauchie MacIntyre, contentedly seated in a pool of water, and fumbling about his pockets in search of his pipe; while the man who stood by him (it was Red Murdoch, but he was not of Allan's acquaintance) was gazing out seaward, with a hand held over one of his eyes, doubtless in the hope of re-ducing to their real number the sailing lights of the rescuing steamer. But the young girl from Kilree?—how was he to discover which she was?—for the women were cowering away from the blast, their faces mostly hidden.

"Is there one Barbara Maclean?" he made bold to ask.

"I am here," said one of those dark figures, in a timid and tearful voice; and at once he went up to her.

"There's a few things here that your aunt and your cousin have sent out to you," said he, "and I am sure you will be glad of them, for the night is so wet. Yes, indeed, now," he went on, "you must take off your shawl, and I will put it over my arm, and here is a dry one. And here is a muffler to go round your neck, and a pair of mittens for your hands. For you must not think they were forgetting you—neither Mrs. Maclean nor Jessie would be likely to do that——"

"I am far aweh from my own home," the girl said, with a sob.

"Oh, yes, yes," said he, in a kindly fashion, "but you are going to another home, and a very friendly home. They could not come out to you; but they let me bring these things out to you; and I am glad to find that matters are no worse. For we will soon have you on board the lighter now, and you will be quite safe."

In common circumstances he was inordinately shy with women; but this poor

creature was quite supine and helpless; and
in her eyes—those beautiful Highland eyes—
large, dark-blue, with raven-black lashes—
there were piteous tears. He treated her as
if she were a child. By the aid of the nearest
lamp, he got out these dry wraps, and sub-
stituted them for her clinging wet shawl; he
made her put the muffler round her neck,
and the mittens on her hands; and then
he said:

"Now maybe we will get away in the
next boat—or at least you will. And mind
your footing. Do not move on the seaweed
—do not move until you find that your feet
are on the limpets."—As if it were necessary
to teach a West Highland girl how to cross
a slippery rock!

However, they struggled along and reached
the water's edge, and, by favour of Mr.
Stewart, Allan was allowed to accompany
his half-cousin or quarter-cousin in the next
boat returning to the *Firefly*. He talked to
her a little, to give her courage. He assisted
her to get into the plunging and rolling
lighter; and there he guided her aft, and
procured for her a warm and comfortable
seat by the boiler, himself standing by her
side, so as not to take up room. And then

he would have her partake of the little
delicacies that Jess Maclean had sent out
for her; but she only shook her head; and
he was not importunate.

Of a sudden she looked up, timorously.

" Have you the Gaelic ? " she asked.

" Indeed I have ! " said he, answering her
in that tongue.

Instantly a grateful light leapt to her eyes ;
and at the same moment, somehow or other,
she put out her hand, and touched his hand,
as if thereby she was recognising some bond
or current of sympathy between them. It
was a trifling little action, perhaps quite
involuntary and inadvertent, and meaning
nothing at all; but it thrilled him strangely.

" It is my thanks to you," said she, now
speaking in Gaelic—and she had a shy and
softly-modulated voice. " It is not every
one that would be so kind to a stranger."

" But you are no stranger," said the young
schoolmaster, in an encouraging way. " For
it is many a time I have heard the Macleans
speak of you; and besides, I am myself a
relative of yours, though not of the same
name."

And thereupon, to beguile the weary time
of waiting, he began and gave her a few

particulars about himself, and about his relations with the Macleans, and about their ways and modes of life. She did not respond much; but she mutely regarded him now and again. Indeed it seemed as if it was not necessary for her to answer him; her eyes did all that; they were the most wonderful eyes—it was not merely that they were beautiful with a mystic and pathetic beauty, but they appeared capable of saying anything, without a word spoken from her lips. For the most part, however, her expression was grave and diffident, as she looked at him from time to time, and listened.

And at last all the passengers—the captain, mate, and most of the crew were remaining by the stranded steamer—had been rescued from their perilous position and conveyed on board the *Firefly*; the blades of the screw began to slash into the tumbling waves; and the vessel moved slowly forward. No farther adventure befell them until they were all safely landed on Duntroone quay—a sorely wet and bedraggled little assemblage; and although it was now about one o'clock in the morning, there were plenty of anxious friends and relatives waiting to receive and

welcome them. And Mrs. Maclean and Jess
would fain have had Allan Henderson come
into the house and sit down with them at
the cheerful and hospitable board that had
been prepared for the entertainment of their
cousin from the outer isles. But he refused.
For some time back he had been drenched
to the skin ; the only thing now for him was
to speed away home, and get to bed. As
for the drying of his clothes, well, they
would have to take their chance : there was
no means of making up a fire, at this hour,
in these poor lodgings.

CHAPTER VI.

THE DAY AFTER.

NEXT morning opened tranquil and serene;
a few flakes of saffron cloud that hung high
in the heavens hardly moved through the
clear expanse.   The mists were slowly rising
from Mull and Morven, the hill-sides reveal-
ing themselves in hues of ethereal rose-grey,
the snow-sprinkled peaks not yet visible.
From the eastern skies, just over the early
smoke of Duntroone, the golden light of the
dawn went level across the bay, and touched
the tall spars and the hulls of the vessels
moored at Ardentrive, and shone warm along
the olive-green slopes of Kerrara ; while a
small red-sailed boat, coming home from the
cod-fishing, made its appearance at the
point, creeping along through the steel-blue,
rippling sea.

And perhaps it was to refresh his eyes
with these beautiful colours, after the black
visions of the night—or perhaps it was, more
practically, to see what the sun could do in
the way of drying his outer garments—that
Allan Henderson, before beginning his daily
round in the Board School, strolled away
round by the quays, and then made up for
his favourite plateau on the top of the
Gallows Hill. And truly it was a different
scene that now met his eyes! Last night
the solitary and commanding feature in all
the formless gloom was the bold and steady
glare of Lismore lighthouse; now Lismore
lighthouse was an insignificant little grey
object, away at the end of the long, low,
green island; while the important things
were the ranges of the mountains, velvet-soft
in their dappled colours, with faint cloud-
shadows here and there—the wide calm
spaces of the sea, trembling in pale and
liquid azure, with one vivid red spot of a
painted beacon at Kerrara point—the ivied
castle on its picturesque rock—the wintry
woods of green pine and brown larch—the
sunlight glinting cheerfully on this or that
window in the town—the broad sweep of the
bay, with a scarlet-funnelled steamer coming

slowly through the blue, from this lofty
pinnacle looking a mere mite of a thing, with
a touch of white at its bows. A fair picture
—shining, reposeful, benign ; no lurid and
ghastly vision of the night, with black
phantasms huddled together on a cruel rock,
the sombre heavens hurling wind and rain
at them, the roar and whirl of the unseen
surge all around them.

Yet it was to that darker vision, and to
the incidents connected with it, that his mind
would return, with a singular and incomprehensible fascination. He gazed abroad upon
this wide-stretching and placid panorama
with eyes that beheld not. A new element
—a perturbing element—had entered into
his existence ; something he did not understand ; something nevertheless powerful
enough to thrust into the background all his
ordinary hopes and ambitions and anxieties,
his restless speculations, his heroic or de-
spondent forecasts as to the future. What
was this new force, then, that threatened to
upset the whole tenor of his life—distracted
as that had already sufficiently been ? He
knew not ; or he would not confess ; or he
feared to think. Happily he could turn his
back on the enigma ; and was even compelled

to do so; for yonder in the town, overlooking the squalid playground, stood the
dingy grey building where his day's labour
was shortly to begin. And so, with his
brows knit, and his head thrown a little
further forward than usual, the schoolmaster
strode away down from this wooded hill;
and ere long, in that depressing and murmuring room, he had once more taken up his
unloved toil.

It was some hours thereafter, it was about
mid-day, that Lauchie MacIntyre awoke to
find himself in a disused hayloft attached to
the distillery. How he had come thither on
the preceding night he knew not, nor was
there any one to tell him; but that was a
minor question; for it is to be imagined
that as the shoemaker now sat up and looked
about him, there was no more sick and
penitent man, bodily and mentally sick and
sorry, in all the three kingdoms. Where
had he been?—what had he done?—what
money had he spent?—nay, what had become of his companion, Red Murdoch?—Red
Murdoch, who ought to have gone ashore at
Tobermory, but would come on to Salen; and
again, after Salen—well, after Salen it was
difficult to say anything about Red Murdoch:

he seemed to have vanished away in a mysterious manner. Then there was the young girl, Barbara Maclean—and here Long Lauchie's conscience became filled with a vague alarm—what had become of her?—what had he done with her?—whither had she, too, disappeared? He had a dim recollection of her at some point in the Sound of Mull—for the steward had come to ask about some tea for her : perhaps, indeed, the steward had looked after her when the *Sanda* arrived at Duntroone? All the same, as these remorseful pangs kept urging him, it would be better for him to go along to Mrs. Maclean's, just to see how the land might lie.

He rose to his feet with a prolonged sigh that was almost a groan ; and, with his ten trembling fingers acting as an ineffectual brush, he tried to remove from his sodden garments the too evident traces of his having passed the night on an unswept floor. Then he left the loft, and with shaky knees descended the flight of wooden steps—fortunately there was no one about. Finally, summoning to him such air of confidence as he could command, he passed along the main street until he came to Mrs. Maclean's shop, which he entered.

" I hope you are very well the day, Mrs. Maclean," said he, rather nervously.

" Oh, yes, indeed," said the widow with her accustomed cheerfulness. " And you yourself? But you are not looking quite so well. Come away in and sit down—— "

" No, no, thank you," said he, shrinking back from the possibility of meeting strangers.

" There's no one in," said she. " Not even Jessie—Jessie has gone over to the house."

Thus assured he stepped into the little parlour, and she followed him, leaving the door a bit open, in case a customer should appear.

" It's little wonder you should be looking not quite so well," she continued, " after such a night as last night. And you'll just take a little drop of something." With which she went to the cupboard.

Now the very soul of Lauchie was crying aloud and in anguish for a glass of whisky; but sternly he held up his hand.

" No, Mrs. Maclean," said he, " I'll no touch it. I wouldna touch a drop. It's a terrible bad thing, whisky. It's the very curse and ruin of the kintry. If I was having my way, I would shut up every

public-house in the kingdom; ay, and I
would have every distiller put into djile."

All the same, she put the decanter and the
glass on the table—though she did not press
him further.

"And have you got your things come
ashore from the wreck?" she asked.

He looked up, in a dazed and yet cautiously
inquisitive manner.

"Ay: the wreck?" he said.

Had there been a wreck, then? And was
that the cause of Barbara Maclean's vanishing into the unknown? But here was her
aunt sitting quite sprightly and content.
And himself?—if there had been a wreck,
how was he come safely here?

"It must have been a fearful time for you,"
the widow continued, unheeding. "And
how the captain managed to put the *Sanda*
on to the Lady Rock, just passes comprehen-
sion: that's what every one is saying—"

"Was the *Sanda* on a rock?" he demanded,
in a bewildered fashion.

Happily she mistook the question.

"Oh, yes, she's on the rock still—the high
tide has not moved her. But who knows
how long she'll be there, if any rough weather
comes? And they're saying that if she had

struck the rock a few yards to the left, she would not have held at all, but would have gone straight to the bottom. I cannot make it out—for there was no such dreadful bad weather. It was bad weather enough," continued the widow, " that you had out in the west, so I am hearing ; and a bad day for the funeral—with such a long way from the house to the seminary."

"Oh, yes, indeed," said the shoemaker, quickly, for here he was on firmer ground. "Terrible bad weather; aw, terrible bad weather ; and as you say, Mrs. Maclean, a long way from the house to the cemetery——"

A customer entered the shop, and Mrs. Maclean left the parlour. The moment her back was turned Long Lauchie, overcome by the tragic temptation of the opportunity, hastily seized the decanter, with tremulous fingers poured out a glass of whisky, and gulped it down. When she returned he was beginning to feel a bit reassured : if only now he could find out what had become of the young lass Barbara !

" Mrs. Maclean," said he, tentatively, " it was a bad night for a wreck, was it not ?— very wet and uncomfortable—indeed I'm feeling my clothes a wee thing damp even now—— "

"And will you not take a drop of the whisky, then, Lauchlan?" said the widow, considerately.

"Aw, Mrs. Maclean," said the shoemaker, with great solemnity, "that you could propose such a thing, and me just telling you that whisky was the curse of the kintry! You have a bad opinion of me if you think I would be touching any such thing! As sure's death, I would sooner walk bare-foot to the top of Ben Cruachan than drink a glass of whisky. But as I was saying: it was a coarse night—and—and the wreck—ay, at the wreck, now—that young lass, your niece—I hope she had plenty round her——"

"Oh, well, indeed," said Mrs. Maclean, "the bundle that Allan Henderson, the schoolmaster, took out to her, was useful enough, no doubt. And it was a friendly thing of the lad to do, seeing that she was a stranger to him. Oh, yes, he is a good lad, he is a kind-hearted lad, is Allan, though he is very stiff-necked, and proud, and ill to manage at times. And when he brought her ashore last night—or rather this morning—and when he brought her up to the house, he would not come in—no—the stubborn chiel

that he is!—but he half-promised to look in
and see us this evening."

Here, indeed, was welcome news : he began
to feel the world more solid beneath his feet.

"Well, it's very glad I am to hear that
your niece has not suffered anything from
the shipwreck," Lauchie ventured to say,
as he rose to take his departure. "I was
looking after her as well as I could—ay—
but when there is a wreck—a wreck is a bad
thing—a wreck is a terrible bad thing—a
man would forget what his own brother was
like when there's so many running backwards and forwards and mekkin a noise.
And now I must be going home, for they'll
be wondering at not seeing me ahl this
time."

It was an unfortunate admission.

"Were you not home last night, Lauchlan?" the widow said—her eyes attracted
to his clothes, which still showed traces of
the hayloft.

He hesitated.

"Well, well—not exactly," said he. "I
had to pass the night with a friend. He
was very seeck ; and he wanted me to sit up
with him. And I was sitting up with him."

She held the door open for him to pass.

"You'll not take a dram?" said she, finally.

"No, no," he made answer, shaking his head. "No. It would be a bad encouragement for ithers. There's no sich things as that for me." And therewithal he said good-bye, and left the shop, and got out into the open day, his eyes blinking at the stronger light. And perhaps he did go home.

Meanwhile Jess, in her gentle and almost motherly way, had taken under her charge the solitary creature who had been confided to their care; and very glad was she to find that her cousin had suffered but little from her recent experiences: no doubt the island-nurtured frame of the girl was pretty well used to cold and wet and considerable spells of fasting. Moreover Barbara Maclean did not at all appear to be too grievously overwhelmed by her bereavement; she hardly ever referred to her father or the funeral; at the present moment, in truth, she seemed mostly concerned about the wooden chest which contained all her little belongings and which had been left on board the *Sanda*.

"But you are sure to get it to-day, Barbara," Jess said, in her persuasive tones.

" The lighter is bringing everything ashore
from the wreck ; and they will send your
box up to you. And in the meantime here
are my things, and you are welcome to choose
just whatever you like."

The large, dark-blue, pathetic eyes of the
girl had been drawn to the two white strips
that terminated Jess's sleeves.

" Would you lend me a pair of cuffs like
them ? " said she—rather slowly, for her
English was not fluent. " I was never
seeing such beautiful ironing. And do you
wear cuffs like that all through the week,
and every day in the week ? "

" Why not ? " said Jess, with a laugh. " I
iron them myself. But I will give you a far
nicer pair of cuffs than these, Barbara, yes,
and a set of tortoise-shell sleeve-links. For,
you see, Allan Henderson, that brought you
home last night, he is coming in this evening,
and perhaps Mr. McFadyen, a friend of ours,
as well ; and you must be looking very nice
and smart. And I am sure you will give
a word of thanks to Allan, for his kindness
of last night. He is rather a shy and proud
and sensitive lad, and not caring to say much
for himself before strangers ; and a word of
thanks would please him, I am sure of that.

Mind this. Barbara, it is not every one that Mr. Stewart would have allowed to go out with him in the lighter; so you were fortunate to have some one to look after you on such a night."

For a second the beautiful eyes of the girl—that seemed to say so much, even when they were really saying nothing at all—were raised to her companion's face; but presently she had withdrawn them, inattentive.

"Will you be going out now, Jessie?" said she. "And will you walk down to the quay, until I see if my box is come over from the wreck?"

Jess at once and good-naturedly assented; they made such trifling preparations as were necessary; and in a short space of time the two cousins were passing along the main street of Duntroone.

CHAPTER VII.

A CEILIDH.

EVENTUALLY the box was found and sent along to the house; and, on the return of the two girls, it was opened; and Jess Maclean was somewhat diffidently invited to look over her cousin's small stock of millinery treasures. These were not sumptuous; for the most part they had been procured at the solitary 'merchant's' shop in Kilree, where feminine finery had to be sought for amidst a heterogeneous display of brown soap, candles, figs, sweetmeats, patent starch, paraffin lamps, and the like; they had seen a good deal of weather out there in the west; and now, as Barbara produced them for inspection, it was with a growing sense of disappointment.

"Everything you have seems so neat and

clean and so stiffly-ironed," she said to her cousin, almost resentfully.

"Well, then," said Jess, with the utmost good-nature, "you must just take any of my things that are of use to you. And especially when there are visitors coming to the house—— "

"They will be thinking I should be in mourning," said Barbara.

"And I am sure they will think nothing of the kind!" responded Jess. "They know, as the rest of us know, that it is very easy for rich people to buy black silks and black bonnets and things of that kind; but it is not so easy for poorer people; and where could any one get mourning at Knockalanish? As for Allan Henderson, the schoolmaster," Jess went on, with a demure laugh, "it is of little consequence what you wear. He would never see it. If you were dressed as a beggar in the streets, or like the Queen on her throne, he would not know the difference. When he fixes those great eyes of his on you —like burning coals—it isn't your dress he is heeding: he is trying to understand what you are thinking—that is all he cares about."

"You talk a good deal about the school-master, Jessie," observed Barbara.

Jess Maclean flushed quickly, and turned her head away ; but she betrayed no anger.

"I think that every one will be talking of him," said she, quietly, " before many years are over."

And thus it was with Jessie's help, and with the loan of a few trifling articles of adornment, that the Highland cousin was got ready for the evening, and very smart and trim and effective she looked. She was indeed a beautiful creature, quite apart from those wonderful, mysterious, appealing eyes ; her features were refined, and even distinguished ; she had the fresh, clear, healthily-tinted complexion that not unfrequently in the western isles is found in conjunction with raven-black hair ; and when she moved, her step was graceful. Her hands, it is true, bore evidence of rough kitchen-work ; but she did not seem conscious of this defect ; nay, she appeared rather inclined to put them forward a little, so that she could better admire the pair of extremely pretty cuffs and the tortoiseshell links that Jess had given her.

Of the two visitors the first to arrive was Mr. Peter McFadyen, who, for a second or so, on being introduced to the stranger, was somewhat disconcerted and taken aback. For this was not at all the mere crofter's lass he had expected to meet—this young lady in becoming attire, whose manner, if shy and reserved, at least betrayed no great embarrassment. But Peter prided himself on being a man of the world; he had soon recovered his self-confidence; he would hear from herself further details of the shipwreck; and, finding that she was somewhat silent— the conversation being now in English—he proceeded to give authoritative views on tides, currents, beacons, and the proper navigation of Duntroone harbour, yet with a touch of jocosity now and again, to show his lightness of heart. Barbara Maclean listened mutely, and sometimes she looked at her cuffs.

Then the blithe little widow appeared, the shop having been shut; and she was almost immediately followed by the young schoolmaster, who, after having gravely greeted these friends, seemed in a measure disposed to keep away from this newly-found half-cousin of his. He sate somewhat removed; and if by chance, or by some subtle instinct, his eyes were raised to regard the face of the girl, they were almost instantly withdrawn,

as if he were afraid. Of course this was
Mr. McFadyen's opportunity. With these
women-folk to impress, he was called upon
for display; he was determined to shine; he
would show them he could talk about other
matters than golf. And now—while Mrs.
Maclean was stirring up the fire to briskness,
and Jess was laying the snow-white table-
cloth—it was the marvels of modern science
that he had got on to; and in particular he
was informing them—as if the illustration
were his own—of the astronomers having
brought within their ken stars so distant
that if, on the day of the battle of Waterloo,
news of the victory could have been dispatched to one of these suns, the telegram
would not even now have arrived.

"Ay, and that's not all!" he exclaimed—
as a premonitory odour of minced collops
and onions wandered in from the kitchen.
"They're saying there's no end—no end to
the universe—you might go on for ever and
ever and only come to more worlds and more
worlds, and more space and more space—
infinite space—infinite—Just think of it—
isn't it terrible to realise——"

"But you can't realise it," said Allan,
with a touch of his scornful impatience.

"You can't what?" demanded the town-councillor.

"It is unthinkable," said the schoolmaster, briefly. "The mind cannot conceive the idea of infinite space."

"Ah?" said Mr. McFadyen, with an inquiring glance. "Ah? You've got to imagine a boundary?—You can't help thinking of a boundary? Is that it?"

"Yes, but you're no further forward that way either," said the younger man, imperturbably. "For you can't imagine a final boundary: if you think of a boundary you must think of something outside the boundary: you build a wall, but there must be something outside the wall as well as in. And so it goes on; and the mischief is that you can neither think of space having an end nor yet of its being endless——"

Peter looked a little dazed—and also suspicious; but he solved the difficulty by breaking into a loud laugh.

"Is that metapheesics?" he cried. "Is that metapheesics, Allan? Dod, man, you're a clever chiel; and the School Board 'll have to be raising your salary! An annual increment of £5 is no half enough."

"I'm sure I'm not caring how many worlds

there are," said the contented little widow,
as she brought the cruet-stand and put it on
the table. "This is the only one that's
handy; and I doubt whether a better one
ever was made. Draw in your chair, Barbara,
my lass; and you, Allan; and you, Mr.
McFadyen. It is well for us that we are
under a roof, and with a good fire—and not
out on the Lady Rock."

Minced collops and onions, a dish of
spinach garnished with boiled eggs, and
bottled stout: these were the materials of
the repast; and a bountiful feast it must
have appeared in the eyes of the young lass
from the Knockalanish croft. The gay little
widow proved a pertinacious hostess; she
would take no refusals, would make no
concessions to shamefacedness; '*what's good
for the Jura factor will do no harm to Fleecy
M'Phail*,' she said, as she helped herself and
others, with here a rallying word, and there
a friendly remonstrance. Indeed this small
party that had been brought together to give
Barbara Maclean a welcome on her home-
coming performed its duty well; surely she
must have perceived that it was not amongst
strangers she had fallen; only the young
schoolmaster remained somewhat aloof and

reserved, and of him she did not take much
notice. Then again, when Mrs. Maclean, in
her frank and off-hand way, came to discuss
the girl's position and prospects, she showed
a tact that she had not always at command.
She would not have Barbara look upon
herself in the light of a dependent. Not at
all. Serious duties would be expected of her.
She would have to manage this house, for
example—the young thing Kirsty was hardly
to be trusted. And there was more than
that. It appeared that the Macleans, mother
and daughter, were in the habit of contract-
ing with the tobacco-manufactory for considerable quantities of Lurgan twist; and
this they dispatched in lesser consignments
to the 'merchants' in the outer isles. The
correspondence attached to this part of the
business was carried on by Jess; but Jess
knew little Gaelic, and could write none at
all; whereas, now, if Barbara would undertake to translate these letters into Gaelic, it
would be a great advantage and recom-
mendation to a good many of the customers
with whom English was practically a foreign
tongue. And what had Barbara to say to
all this?

"I am sure," the girl said, speaking rather

slowly, as was her wont, " that I am very
willing to do anything that I can do. But
I cannot write the Gaelic. I know it very
well—oh, yes—better than English a great
deal ; but I have never tried to write it. It
was always English they were having in the
school at Kilree."

And now, and almost for the first time
this evening, Allan Henderson addressed
her.

" If that is all," said he, " there is no
trouble. It would be a very easy thing for
you to learn the Gaelic spelling, when you
know the language well. You would not
find it very difficult, after you had got the
rules." He hesitated—for the large, beautiful
eyes were regarding him calmly, perhaps
even curiously. " If you would like," he
went on, " I would come along in the evening
to give you some lessons. An hour each
evening would do. It is a pity you should
know Gaelic so well, and not be able to
write it."

She did not answer him at the moment :
it was Jess Maclean who looked up, startled.
For could this really be Allan Henderson,
who ordinarily was so backward, or impatient,
or scornfully indifferent wherever young

women were concerned, yet who now proposed to devote an hour each evening in the
week to this solitary converse? And that
was most assuredly what this private tuition
would mean. No one else wanted to learn
Gaelic spelling. And would the class, consisting of teacher and pupil, be held in the
house here, while she and her mother would
be over the way in the shop?

At this point Peter McFadyen interposed
in a stormily goodhumoured fashion.

"Mrs. Maclean," he cried, "I call you to
order. Surely there has been enough of
business—enough of business; and I would
not have Miss Barbara bothered with threats
of lessons the moment she sets foot in your
house. It's all very well for you, Allan, my
lad; every one to his trade; but at the
proper time; and the proper time is not
every time. No, no; there are other things;
there are amusements; we cannot have all
work and no play; I may not be very well
skilled in metapheesics, but I know when we
should have a dance and a song and a merry-
making, to keep the game of life going.
And let me see: what is there to the fore
now—— "

He appeared to be summoning up to his

mind the innumerable gaieties of Duntroone in the winter.

" Well, now, for example, there's the Gaelic Choir to-morrow night—the practising in the Drill-Hall—and we could not do better than go there, to hear the practising for Mrs. McAskill's soree. I'm going ; I must go ; I must make my voice heard to-morrow evening——— "

" Oh, are you going to sing, Mr. Mc-Fadyen ? " said the widow, encouragingly.

" To sing ? " he repeated. " Well—well—no—for I am not one of the Choir. But as for a song," he proceeded, refusing to confess himself abashed, " if it is a song you would like, well, when we are round the fire in a little while, I will try a song, just as if we were at an old-fashioned *ceilidh*.* There is not half enough of spirit among the younger men of the present day——— "

" And do you call yourself anything else than one of the younger men ! " the widow protested, in a kind fashion.

" Why, in the former days," continued Mr. McFadyen, affecting not to have overheard this agreeable compliment, " when you were at supper, and there were fowls at supper,

* *Ceilidh*—a friendly gathering.

and if you found a particular bone, you would send it to such or such a one, and he would have to make verses in Gaelic there and then. So I have heard. I am not good at the Gaelic myself; but as for a song, I would not spoil any merry party by refusing —not at all! And what I was saying was this—to-morrow night, when the Gaelic Choir are at the Drill-Hall, I am going to put a question to them; I am indeed. What kind of songs are they going to sing at Mrs. McAskill's soree—that's what I want to know. Dod's bless my soul, is there any use in being muzzerable? Is there any use in being muzzerable, Mrs. Maclean?—"

"Well, I never found any myself," said the little widow, suavely. "And I'm told that giving way to it is fearfu' bad for the congestion——"

"There's some truth in that anyway," observed the schoolmaster, in a kind of grim undertone.

"Now what's the favourite songs all through the West Highlands?" demanded Peter, indignantly. "I'll tell you, then. There's three in particular. There's the *Fear a Bhata*—the Farewell to the Boatman; there's the Farewell to Fuinary; there's Farewell to Mackrimmon—all of them Farewells; and are we to have nothing but Farewells and Farewells and Farewells, when a few friends have met together, to pass a merry hour or two? And I know the Choir have plenty of other songs. I can see them in their own books. If I cannot make quite clear sense out of the Gaelic, at least I can read the translation; and there's plenty of sensible songs, instead of Farewells and Farewells."

He suddenly turned to his neighbour.

"Miss Barbara," said he, "do you know the '*Return, my darling*'?"

The colour came swiftly to the face of the young Highland girl on her being thus unexpectedly addressed.

"No I do not," she said, with downcast eyes.

"It is the *O, till, a leannain*, Barbara," said Jess—who was a member of the Choir.

"Well, now, there is a sensible song!" continued McFadyen, with spirit. "Some night I will sing it to you—at present I am not sure of the air. But listen to words like this—

' *If you on my dear one should gaze, should gaze,*
If you were to hear what she says, she says,
If you heard my pretty
One singing her ditty
Your bosom would get in a blaze, a blaze.'

That's sense. That's sensible. That doesna belong to the devil's clan of Farewells! And I must make my voice heard to-morrow evening at the Choir—oh, yes, indeed. We are going to have a merry evening at Mrs. McAskill's—and it is useless lamenting for Mackrimmon, and Mackintosh, and Lovat, and the rest of them. And sure I am that if Miss Barbara here will go with us, there will be an invite for her too; yes, yes; Mrs. McAskill is an old friend of mine; and my friends are her friends. We'll make up a little party, and we'll all go together; and I'm thinking it might be just as well if I brought a machine."

Nor did Peter, in his determination to keep things going gaily, forget his promise about singing them a song, when they had left the table and were seated in a cosy semicircle round the fire. The others had forgotten, it is true; for Allan Henderson had chanced to ask of the widow the origin of a saying she had accidentally used—'Step for step to thee, old woman, and the odd step to Ewen'; and she was telling them the story: how Ewen Cameron of Lochiel was returning home late one night; how he was followed by a witch, who tried to overtake

him; how he made use of this phrase,
and held on his way successfully, keeping
one step in advance of her, until he reached
the ferry; how he had jumped into the boat,
while the ferryman drove the witch-hag back;
how she had called to Lochiel 'My heart's
desire to thee, dear Ewen!' and how he,
divining her purpose, had called in return
'Thy heart's desire to the big rock yonder'—
whereupon the big rock split into two pieces,
visible even unto this day at Ballachulish
Ferry. To all this Jess listened half-laugh-
ing—she was familiar with most of her
mother's old-world sayings and tales; but
Barbara's eyes were intent and awe-stricken;
and it was the expression of her face, rather
than the legend, that held the schoolmaster's
attention fascinated and enthralled. Of
course the town-councillor was too polite to
interrupt. But as soon as Mrs. Maclean had
finished her narrative, he put his hand over
his mouth and coughed significantly.

"It is not so easy," said he, "to sing without an accompaniment; but a promise is a
promise; and I will do my best."

Whereupon he began, in a curious falsetto
voice that seemed to come from just behind
his teeth, instead of from his chest or throat:

‘ The sun has gane down o’er the lofty Ben Lomond ’

—this was his song; and he was evidently
proud of his performance; for he took
plenty of time, and introduced all manner of
ornate trills of execution, that could only
have been acquired by long practice—

‘ And left the red clouds to preside o’er the scene,
While lanely I stray in the calm simmer gloamin’,
To muse on sweet Jessie, the flower o’ Dumblane.’

The dog!—pretending to sing the praises
of Jessie the Flower of Dumblane, when it
was as clear as noonday that it was Jessie
the Flower of Duntroone he had in his mind.
However, there was no covert look or smile;
it was too serious a matter for that; for now
when he came to the second half of the verse
he fairly outdid himself—those flourishes and
grace-notes were so abundant that the tune
got hopelessly lost amongst them—never had
words been so embroidered—

‘ How sweet is the brier, wi’ its saft faulding blossom,
And sweet is the birk, wi’ its mantle o’ green ;
Yet sweeter and fairer, and dear to this bosom,
Is lovely young Jessie, the flower o’ Dumblane.
Is lovely young Jessie, Is lovely young Jessie,
Is lovely young Jessie, the flower o’ Dumblane.’

Nay, when he arrived at the final repetition
of the phrase ‘ lovely young Jessie ’—which

is rather high-pitched in the music, he
actually opened his mouth, and the consequence was a prolonged and shrill scream :
indeed, so effective and overwhelming was
the climax of this last line that the widow,
carried away by her enthusiasm, called out
'Well done!—well done!' and clapped her
hands.

"Mother," said Jess, blushing furiously,
" there's more verses !"

"No, no," said Mr. McFadyen, modestly,
" I'll not sing any more the night. I got
into rather a high key—and—and my voice
is a little out of practice—— "

" You did well—you did just famously ! "
the widow maintained. But Peter had given
evidence of his possession of musical powers,
and was blandly satisfied.

Altogether it appeared to be a very happy
evening for every one concerned, though, to
be sure, the young girl from the outer isles
remained distant and silent. And to the
young schoolmaster that silence of hers was
far more impressive than anything else could
have been ; it accorded with a certain inde-
finable quality, a certain mysterious element
of remoteness that seemed to surround her.
And what was the origin, he asked himself

as he wandered away homeward through the
sleeping town—but not to his books; his
thoughts were too perturbed and quick-
changing for any application to books—what
was the origin of this strange influence she
appeared to convey, even without a single
spoken word ? Was it the mere sense of her
loneliness ? Or had it anything to do with
the circumstances in which he had first
encountered her—finding the solitary and
forsaken creature on that black reef, with
the darkness all around, and the noise of
hurrying waters ? And what was it that
her eyes said, that no mortal eyes had ever
said to him before ? Those beautiful blue
deeps under the raven lashes—so calm, so
still, so mystic in their very apathy—did
they not bring some revelation, some message
wholly apart from mere human emotions and
affections ?

"They seem to speak of the sea and of the
night," he said to himself, in the long and
sleepless hours of recalling and remembering.

CHAPTER VIII.

BARBAROSSA.

THE very next day, to Jess Maclean's astonishment, Allan Henderson walked into the shop: it was a most unusual hour for him to make an appearance.

"There is a half-holiday at the school," he said, "the Head-Master has had great news about his son who is at Oxford. And I was thinking, Jessie, if you were free for an hour or so, you might like to go across to Kerrara, and climb up the hill, and find out if anything further has happened to the *Sanda*. I have got Angus MacIsaac's boat—it's down at the slip——"

Jess Maclean's kindly grey eyes were lit up with pleasure: in Duntroone it is a special compliment and mark of favour for a young man to ask a young woman to go for a row with him. And this suggestion about the *Sanda* was obviously the merest excuse : every one knew what was happening to the *Sanda*; she was found to be irremovably jammed on to the rock, and irretrievably damaged; and the steam-lighter was kept engaged in bringing ashore any of her fittings that might be of value—before the next gale came along to hammer her to bits.

" Well, I am not so busy," said Jess, laying down her book-keeping pen. " There is little doing at this time of the year."

" And would your cousin Barbara care to go too ? " the young schoolmaster added, somewhat diffidently.

The light vanished from Jess Maclean's face.

" I should think that Barbara had had enough of boats for a while," she said, somewhat coldly.

Yet she was the soul of goodhumour and unselfishness. The hurt and disappointed look did not last a second. Was it to be wondered at that he should have conceived a sudden interest in this beautiful creature who had come into their little circle, and who had, by fortune of accident, made especial claim on his attention and pity ?

" Barbara ?" said Jess, after a moment, in
her usual bland way. " Oh, yes, indeed, I
am sure she will be glad to go ; and I will
run across the way and tell her—if you will
step into the parlour and talk to my mother
for a moment or two, while Barbara and I
are getting ready." For there was no kind
of grudging in this woman's nature : if it
was really on account of Barbara that he had
made this proposal—well, Barbara was the
more fortunate.

Now Barbara did not respond to this
invitation with the gratitude that might have
been expected ; but Jess at last induced her
to go ; and when both the girls were ready,
they crossed over to the shop, and Allan and
they proceeded down to the beach, where the
boat was awaiting them. They took their
places in the stern ; he followed in, and got
hold of the oars ; then they shoved off, and
he set out to pull them across the bay. On
the whole it was a most auspicious start ; for
if the morning had been somewhat squally,
all the world was now a blaze of splendour ;
the Mull mountains, clear to the top, were of
an almost summer-like blue ; summer-like
was the blue of the lapping and flashing
waters around them ; while between these

brilliant breadths of colour ran the long spur
of Kerrara, its russet and russet-yellow slopes
basking in the sun.   It is true that Jess,
knowing the climate, had brought a thick
plaid with her; it now lay unheeded over
their knees.

And for a considerable time all went well,
and they made good progress across to the
island.   Allan was a capable oarsman; the
tall young schoolmaster, despite his slight
stoop, possessed a wiry frame; and everybody along this coast can handle a boat.
But by-and-bye, and almost imperceptibly,
the aspect of things began to alter a little.

" Allan," said Jess, " I think we are going
to have a shower."

" No, no—no shower," said he, confidently;
for of course he was looking back to the
land—and there all was placid sunlight, from
the white houses dotted along the terraced
cliffs out to the ivied castle at the point.

Jess laughed.

" Allan," said she, " where is the island of
Mull ? "

He turned his head.   There was no island
of Mull.   The mountains of tender, ethereal
rose-purple and azure had all disappeared;
and in their place there was a far-stretching

film of silvery-grey, entirely shutting out the world beyond.

"And what's that down the Sound?" Jess demanded again.

He turned and looked in the other direction. Off the mouth of Loch Feochan a broad black band lay on the water—a band of almost inky hue; but even as they regarded it, it began to resolve itself—it came creeping stealthily along, leaving a vague indistinctness in its wake. Then Kerrara itself appeared to undergo gradual transformation; the low-lying hills took loftier and mystic forms; through this ever-advancing veil they looked strange and remote. And was there not some darkness assembling overhead?—some pervading gloom all around? The blue had gone from the sea.

"Quick!—quick!" cried Jess—and she opened out the thick plaid and threw it round Barbara and herself, the two of them crouching together, their heads bent down.

Then with a cold and angry swirl of wind came the first rattle of the rain—splashing on thwarts and gunwale, and hissing on the leaden sea; the gloom around them increased; the island they were making for seemed to recede and recede, until it appeared to be a hopeless distance away; and then again—in about another couple of minutes—they could descry that same island of Kerrara shining a beautiful golden-green behind the grey folds of the wet; the world lightened and still further lightened; and as they once more emerged into blue water and warm sunshine, behold! the mountains of Mull had returned —the velvet-hued shoulders of purple and soft rose-grey showing along their summits a slight sprinkling of snow, left by the swift-drifting shower.

And now they were come to Ardentrive, the solitary and secluded bay in which the yachts of this part of the coast are laid up for the winter. Very forlorn and ghostly looked those silent, dismantled vessels; yet they were interesting in a way; it was like walking past empty rooms, thinking of vanished glories. And as they went from one to the other, Allan chanced to notice that the gangway of a certain schooner had not been properly fixed down.

"Would you like to go on board and have a look about the deck?" said he to his companions. "It would not be difficult."

"If you're sure there's no one on the yacht," said Jess, doubtfully.

"There cannot be," he pointed out. "There's no boat astern. And who would be on board a yacht at this time of year?"

And yet, when at length he had clambered over the gunwale, and opened the gangway, and had got the two girls hauled up on deck, and when they began to peer about, there were some unusual symptoms observable.

"I never saw a boat left like this," said he—for everybody in Duntroone knows something about boats. "Look at the tarpaulin of the skylight—it has been taken off and thrown back again; what is to prevent a gust of wind from blowing it overboard?"

He pursued his investigations.

"Look here," he called again, "the doors of the companion-way have been left open. Let us go down and see the saloon!"

He shoved back the hatch of the companion-way, and proceeded to descend the steps, the two girls rather timorously following. Indeed there was something uncanny in finding themselves in possession of this deserted ship; moreover, beneath them was a vague and mysterious gloom, for the tarpaulin, loose as it might be, quite sufficiently covered the deck skylight.

But the next moment this indefinite apprehension had given way to the most violent alarm and terror. For no sooner had Allan reached the open door of the saloon than he suddenly stopped short, and instinctively threw out both arms, as if to bar the further progress of the women.

"What in the name of God is that!" he exclaimed, gazing with awe-stricken eyes into the dim obscurity.

"It's a dead man!" cried Barbara, with a piercing shriek. "Come away — Jess! — Jess!"

But Jess was too terrified to move: she could only stare into the semi-darkness at the ghastly object that there presented itself. And Allan, also, stood and stared—wondering whether they had stumbled into dreamland, and broken in upon the slumbers of the Emperor Barbarossa. For at the further end of the sombre saloon, half-reclining against the cushions, and apparently dead asleep, there was an upright figure clad in a white mantle; some kind of crown surmounted his brows; and on the table before him lay a metal instrument, brass or gold it seemed to be in the prevailing dusk. The red-bearded sleeper did not stir or show any sign of life; and the silence around him was as the silence of the grave.

"Jess!—Jess!" said Barbara, with ashen lips. "Come away—it is a work of the devil!"

But Jess, trembling though she was, would not leave Allan; she felt safer standing by him than in trying to flee from the neighbourhood of that appalling phantasm; unknown to herself she had put her hand on the young man's arm, and would have dragged him back, when he advanced a step.

"Who are you?—and what are you?" he demanded, in a loud voice.

The white figure slowly moved; a pallid face appeared to regard the intruders; then of a sudden the unknown snatched up the sceptre-looking instrument that lay on the table, and brandished it before him.

"Away, away!" he called shrilly, in Gaelic. "It's I that will not be satisfied till the Bay of Duntroone is filled with blood— with blood!—with blood! Ten thousand down from the Gallows Hill—ten thousand hurled over the Minard cliffs—sweep them, sweep them into the sea—till they know the power of the King! The power of the King!—that must walk on the neck of his enemies, and splash the lintels of his door with their blood, till not one of them be left in the land! Hurl them over—crush them —mangle them—slaves, away now, and do my bidding!—for the bloody slaughter shall not cease till the going down of the sun!— "

In his frantic gesticulation, the red beard, which was merely a strip of cow's hide, got disarranged, and fell to the floor.

" It's Niall Gorach,* " cried Jess, in amazement.

But the poor half-witted lad, hearing this real voice, began dimly to perceive that these strangers were actual human beings, not the ghosts and hallucinations he had been accustomed to command, in his madder moments, from this throne of state. He peered curiously at them, in a frightened way, and now he was all trembling.

" Have you come for me ? " he said, in pitiful and whimpering tones — and he humbly laid down his sceptre, which was none other than the brass poker belonging to the stove.

" Why, how did you get here ? " demanded Allan.

* Half-witted Neil.

"I took a boat from the Corran shore," he answered—looking furtively and apprehensively from one to the other in this obscure twilight.

"And where did you get the oars for her?"

"I took a piece of wood from the Dunchoillie fence — and — and I watched the tides."

"And what have you done with her now?"

"I shoved her away."

"And left yourself to starve! Why, how long have you been on board this yacht?"

"I am not knowing—a long time, I think— many thousands of people were coming to see me——" But here he checked himself; his visionary kingdom was over; and the world of fact and substance had found him.

"And have you had anything to eat and drink?"

"I brought a bag of meal and a cask of water," he said; and then he added, in an appealing way: "I will give you some if you will not hurt me, or put me in jail." Nay, so abject and penitent was he, that he took the tinselly crown from his forehead and timidly placed it on the table: it was the last sign and symbol of his abdication.

Well, they were not disposed to be too

hard on the poor wretch, whose royal govern-
ment of spectral armies, in this solitary cabin,
could not have done much harm to anybody ;
and, indeed, as it turned out, Niall was the
means, the unintentional means, of doing
Allan Henderson an excellent good turn this
afternoon. For of course they had to take
him with them—after they had dispossessed
him of his blanket-robe and returned it to a
locker, and after they had shut up and
made secure everything on board the yacht
as well as they could, with some comments
on the negligence of caretakers. Then they
pulled ashore and landed on Kerrara, leaving
Niall in charge of the boat drawn up on the
beach. They next proceeded to climb the
nearest hill from which they might have a
view of the distant Lady Rock, this being
the ostensible aim of their excursion. It
was, in truth, very little they could see of
the unfortunate *Sanda* beyond a touch of red
that revealed her funnel ; however, they had
come to look at the steamer ; and, now that
they had accomplished their object, there was
nothing for them but to go away home again
—Allan could find no further excuse for pro-
longing this all too delightful lingering and
its secret and magnetic association.

Of a sudden Jess Maclean, who was a sharp-eyed lass, began to giggle, and then to laugh outright.

" Do you know what has happened ? " she said. " Where is your boat, Allan ? "

The schoolmaster wheeled round. There was no doubt about what had happened. The young rascal Niall, seizing his opportunity, had shoved off, jumped into the boat, and was now making for the mainland, as hard as ever he could pull.

" The scoundrel ! " said Allan—not a little disconcerted. " But it is no matter. Angus MacIsaac will catch him when he gets ashore, and Angus will bring the boat back for us."

" Oh, do you think so ? " said Jess, with merriment in her pretty grey eyes. " Well, now, do you see where the daft lad is going ? For he is not so daft as to try landing at the quay or any of the slips ; no, no ; he is making for the little bay at Dunchoillie, and as soon as he has got ashore, he will escape away through the woods. Allan, how many miles is it we'll have to walk to the ferry ? "

Clearly this was now what stared them in the face. Other hope for them there was none. They waited a long time to see if any sane creature should chance to capture the runaway, and have the understanding to send back the boat; but nothing of the kind occurred; and so they set out—Allan secretly rejoicing—to walk away over the rough island to the ferry that crosses Kerrara Sound.

He bore Niall no ill-will for having played them this trick. The world was full of wonder and a subtle fascination all through the hours of this enchanted afternoon; and when eventually they got across to the mainland there were more of magic spells; for they walked home through a lambent twilight, with a crescent moon of clear gold nearly overhead; while far away in the west, high above the mystic glooms and phantom-shapes of the Mull hills, there was a stormy glare of rose-pink, that sent a warm flush across the now approaching Duntroone, its houses, and woods, and scant gardens. Yes, and all his life seemed likewise to have burst into flame: whether a consuming flame it was for the inscrutable Fates to determine and declare.

CHAPTER IX.

PROBLEMS AND DREAMS.

Now on the Sabbath day it was the custom of the good folk of Duntroone, excepting the ultra-strict amongst them, to permit themselves a little walk along the sea-front after morning service; and this was the next opportunity to which the schoolmaster could look for resuming—without any appearance of intrusive haste—his acquaintance with the wonderful stranger from the outer isles: perchance in the vague hope of inveigling Jess and her to go with him for some brief landward stroll. But alas! for these fond desires. On the Saturday evening there was a filmy and mysterious halo round the crescent moon; an hour or two later the wind began to rise—with a vague premonitory howl; before midnight a full gale was raging,

shaking the house to its very foundations ;
and through the long dark there was a
clattering of windows and a succession of
deluges of rain that told of what was happening outside. Then his first despairing
glimpse of the new day seemed to say that
all was over. The driven and turbulent sea
was of a livid green, with the white crests of
the chasing waves whirled aloft and scattered
in spindrift ; the water was surging heavily
along the quays and springing high in foam ;
the roadways were deep in mud ; and a
solitary pedestrian, a woman, with her head
butted down, and her ineffectual waterproof
blown up into a black balloon, was being
dragged hither and thither as she strove
against the gusts of the storm. A cheerless
prospect, truly ; for Duntroone, on a wet
Sunday, is the wettest-looking place in all
the wild and wet West Highlands.

Nevertheless, the weather was not likely
to imprison the young schoolmaster ; out-of-
doors could be no colder than this fireless
and miserable room of his ; besides, he was
restless, ill-at-ease, and longing to be away in
free and open solitude ; and so, making some
inward excuse about having a look round
to see if there was any chance of the day

bettering, he set forth, and eventually found himself climbing to the summit of the Gallows Hill. There he made sure he would have all the world to himself alone.

But it was not so. To his astonishment he discovered that he had been forestalled. Lauchie MacIntyre, the shoemaker, was seated on the bench at the foot of the flag-staff.

" Well, Lauchlan," said he, " you're early astir. And what's brought you up here?"

" My head is not so well," said Lauchlan, sadly, and he took his cap off and laid it on his knees. " And I thought there would be a fine cold wind blowing on the hill."

" Maybe you had a little drop last night, then?" Allan suggested.

The melancholy-visaged shoemaker glanced reproachfully at the younger man.

" Aw, Mr. Henderson, that you would think the likes of that of me!—me that's a Rechabite, and was at a Band of Hope meeting only the night before last. There's no such things as that for me—no, no. Now look at this: there's many a man would have tekken to drink long ago in my place. There's many a man would have tekken to drink when his wife run aweh from him.

But not me—not me; says I to myself
' Lauchie, let the duvvle go, and welcome to
her.' And this one and that was saying I
should go through to Fort William, and
bash the head of that little bandy-legged
carpenter; but says I to myself ' No, no; if
he's willing to tek up with a duvvle like
that, it is you, Lauchie, that is well rid of
them both, and be tammed to them !' What
would I be going to Fort William for?
It's not to Fort William I would be going,
when I might have to bring her back
again ! "

" Yes, I've heard you were a married man,"
said Allan, absently. And he did not go on
his way, as he had purposed doing, to secure
silence and solitude for himself. He sate
down on the bench, beside the shoemaker.
For here at least was a human being, who
had come through, in however blind and
bleared a fashion, certain of the great crises
and experiences of life—had perhaps even,
unknown to himself, been face to face with
problems and mysteries. What, for example,
was the origin of this disenchantment and
repulsion that he had so freely confessed ?
And Allan had no fear of making any
humiliating or disturbing discoveries. It

was the truth he wanted, seen from whatever side.   He was well aware that a Sancho
Panza element exists in human nature, and
that not to its detriment : the gargoyle does
not detract from the majesty of the cathedral.

"Yet I warrant," said he to Long Lauchie,
"that you sang a different song when she
was your sweetheart—when you believed her
to be the finest creature in all the country—
when you cared for nothing, for nothing in
the world, so much as to see her eyes look
kindly at you when you came near.   Isn't
that so?   Am I right ? " he went on, seeing
that the dejected shoemaker was silent.   " I'm
thinking there was a time when you wouldn't
have contentedly seen her go away with
another man.   No ; you would rather have
been for breaking the head of any man that
wanted even to be a little friendly with her.
There must have been a time when the
madness was on you.   They tell me that
when a man sees the one woman in all the
world that he must have for his wife, it is
a kind of madness that comes over him——"

"A madness ? " said Lauchlan, gloomily.
" Ay.   There was ten days of it.   Her father
he keepit a public-house in Tobermory ; and
when I came to myself at the end of the ten

days, they were saying that I had promised
to marry Jean. Ay, they were saying that.
And mebbe I had. And mebbe I had not.
But it was of little matter; for her father he
was a decent man; and there was ahlways
a glass for a friend; and there was a talk of
a fine wedding—so I said no more."

Tinkle-tankle—tinkle-tankle went the bell
of the Catholic chapel; and one or two small
dark figures began to appear in the distant
thoroughfares.

"But no doubt you hoped for the best,"
continued Allan. "And what was't, think
you, made the marriage turn out ill?"

"The drink," replied Long Lauchie, with
mournful resignation. "She was just like
the rest. Ahl the weemen are alike. They're
ahl alike. They're ahl at the drink, or
worse. There's a cousin of mine that is a
gamekeeper over on Loch Awe-side, and he
says the two classes that mek ahl the mischief
of the kintry are weemin and meenisters,
and that it's a pity there does not break out
a grouse-disease among them to sweep them
ahl aweh. Ay, indeed."

It was without anger that Lauchlan
delivered himself of these quite desperate
views of life and feminine human nature:

he had escaped from the toils, and was merely a passive spectator now.

"And do you mean to say," Allan demanded, "that you allowed your wife to run away from you without making the least effort to bring her back?"

"Well, now," said the shoemaker, with greater animation, "I will just tell you what happened that day, and I will ask you if I did not do right. I was down at the North Quay, with a friend of mine that was going to Ballachulish, and we were waiting for the *Fusilier* to come over from the South Quay. And when the *Fusilier* was brought alongside, then one of the lads of the steamer he comes running up the gangway, and he says 'Lauchie, do you know that your wife is in the fore-caybin?' 'No,' says I, 'I do not.' 'Well she is,' says he, 'and him that's along with her is MacKillop, the carpenter, from Fort William; and I'm thinking it's not ahl right, from the look of them.' 'And do you tell me now,' says I, 'that my wife is rinning aweh with MacKillop the carpenter?' 'It is not for me to answer such a question,' says he. 'It is for you to come on board and get hold of your wife.' 'Is it?' says I. 'Then I will see her tammed first. If she's rinning aweh with the bandy-legged carpenter, let the duvvle go and welcome!' Then says Johnnie: 'They are carrying a big bundle between them.' Well, at that, Mr. Henderson, at that something came over me. 'Johnnie, lad,' says I, 'come aweh down quick to the fore-caybin, and you'll seize hold of the bundle, and I'll give the carpenter a clout that will mek him think it's the Day of Chidgment.' That's what I was saying; and my foot was on the gangway; but I stopped. Ay, indeed, I stopped. Says I to myself: 'Is it not a good thing to be rid of a lot of weemen's clothes? Does any one want a lot of weemen's clothes hanging about one's house?' And back I stepped from the gangway. 'Let them go to Fort William, or to the duvvle, bundle and all!' says I— and in a few minutes aweh went the *Fusilier*, and I've never set eyes on either of them since. And there's many a man would have made that excuse for tekkin to drink; but I'm not wan of that kind; no, no; I would rather do what little I can to banish ahl that sin and shame from our kintry. Ay, that's jist what it is: drink is the sin and shame of the kintry. Have you a fill of tobacco, Mr. Henderson?"

But Allan had left his pouch behind him. So Lauchie with a patient sigh put his pipe in his pocket again, and rose to his feet.

"I am thinking I will be getting home now. My head is not so well. Mebbe I will try lying down on my bed for a while—there is little hope of meeting in with a friend on a day like this." So Long Lauchie departed; and the young schoolmaster was left alone with this great, wide, far-stretching world of moving shapes and vaporous glooms.

Nevertheless there was still some small glimmering of hope. Occasionally there would come a suffused silvery look into a portion of the eastern skies; the lurid and formless heavens would show symptoms of banking up; while the slopes of Kerrara, catching this or that wandering gleam, would burn an intense russet-yellow against the blue-black of the Mull mountains. Then again a gradual fading of that wild glare; a gathering darkness; an advancing murmur of wind and water; and forthwith a white smoke of rain would go tearing across the bay, the squall whirling onwards with the hurrying waves. There was not a dog visible along all the deserted sea-front of Duntroone.

However, storm or shine, the people would soon be coming out of the churches now, and so he slowly and watchfully made his way downward from these gusty heights. As the first of the worshippers began to appear, he quickened his pace; he would have to intercept the two girls—yet in a casual kind of way; most likely they would make straight for home, instead of attempting any promenade along the wet concrete, that was now all littered with seaweed. And this was precisely what happened. Another minute or two and he would have missed them. He encountered them at the corner of the street. They had had no thought of going along by the sea-front on such a morning.

"Well, now, Allan," said Jess, with her grey eyes smiling benignly (Barbara paid little heed to him : she seemed more concerned about keeping her waterproof-sleeves well over her wristbands) "this is not a day for any one to be outside. Will you come home with us, and take a little bit of dinner with us ?"

"It is very kind of you, Jessie," he was beginning to say, with some embarrassment, when she interrupted him.

"But you are going to refuse, as usual. Do you think it is very friendly, Allan? I know that we cannot talk about anything that would interest you, for the President of the Duntroone Literary and Scientific Society is such a great person; but we would make you welcome; and cousins, cousins in the Highlands especially, should not be so ceremonious."

Well, the President of the Duntroone Literary and Scientific Society might or might not have been a great and learned person; but at least he had not the heart to refuse this cunningly-worded invitation; and the next minute he was accompanying the two girls on their homeward way.

"And who knows," continued Jess, in her kindly fashion, "but that the afternoon may clear up a bit, and Barbara and you and I might go for a walk over to Ganavan? Oh, yes, it is just as likely as not to clear up a little!"

And eventually, as it turned out, her cheerful optimism was rewarded; for by three o'clock the state of affairs looked sufficiently promising to induce them to leave the house; and deep was the joy in Allan's heart when they had actually set forth upon this excursion. They took an inland route to begin with, but it mattered little to him whither they went. Perhaps it was merely chance that placed him by Barbara's side as they started off; at any rate, he found himself once more subject to the overmaster‐ing spell of her mere presence—the inexplic‐able, extraordinary entrancement of being near her—the wonder and delight of being able to regard the wind stirring the wisps and tangles of her raven-black hair. And indeed that was about all of her companion‐ship that she vouchsafed to him. She rarely spoke, except to answer a question: it was Jess who did all the talking, teasing him and mocking him, and yet becoming sym‐pathetic enough when she happened to touch upon anything really affecting himself or his future.

They left the highway—they followed a farm road—crossed some heights and knolls—and came in sight of the western seas again. A sombre day, perhaps, for a country walk; and yet there was plenty of colour in the wintry landscape—the yellow of the pastures, the dank crimson of the withered breckan, the intense green of the whins, the blood-red of the bramble-stems trailing across the swollen brook. And when, as they were descending from the heights towards the shore, a sudden fire broke through the heavy clouds lying over the mountains in Mull, why, all the world around them grew radiant, and even the leafless ash-trees caught something of the welcome light, a shimmering touch of silver on the branches that stretched away up into the leaden-hued sky. A most comforting gleam ; it was full of promise ; it seemed to speak of a general breaking up of those louring heavens : perhaps, by the time they were returning home they might have for company the crescent moon.

At the foot of the hill the burn runs at right angles, and as they were crossing the rude little bridge Allan happened to espy, under the straggling blood-red stems of the brambles, a small white star.

" Why," he said, " there is the first wild-flower I have seen this year ! "

He stepped down the slippery bank, reached under the bushes, and brought away the tiny prize. It was only a daisy—not ' crimson-tipped ' at all—but pale and colourless ; none the less the first timid harbinger of the spring was surely an interesting thing, with its mystic message of wonder and hope.

Then it was in its way a rarity; he was bound to present it to one of his companions. To which of them? Jess rather stood aside a little, looking askance.

" Would you care to have it ? " said he to Barbara, and he shyly offered her this humble little token.

Yes, she took it; and she thanked him in a kind of fashion—that is to say, with her voice, not with any glance of her unfathomable eyes; then they went on again. And Jess had not lingered behind to wipe away any sudden tears of mortification and reproach ; for she was a sensible lass ; and she had but the smallest sense of her own importance and value in the world. Only, for a little time, she was silent and preoccupied.

They went down to the shore, and the sands, and the rocks, round which the dark green sea was monotonously washing, with crisp white flashes of foam here and there. A lonely place ; as the calling of the startled birds bore witness—curlews, oyster-catchers, sandpipers, and the like ; while everywhere there was dispersal—the black and white gleam of a pair of arrow-flighted mergansers, the slow-flapping laboured progress of a heron, the cautious retreat of a deep-swimming skart that was already a mile out from shore, dipping its head from time to time, and paddling still further away. But in a very few minutes silence prevailed again ; several of the flocks of birds returned to their feeding-grounds ; and when the three strangers, having sought out a convenient seat for themselves on the rocks, took their places, there was no further cry or sign of protest against the intrusion.

And of what did these young folk talk, in the gathering twilight ? Allan Henderson hardly knew. The folds of her dress were visible to him, that was enough ; the magnetic, alarming consciousness that she was almost within touch of him ; the secret wistful hope that sooner or later she might turn towards him more friendly, more interested, eyes. It was Jess who rather came to the rescue ; and so also on their way back to the town ; she had heard of the great German mediæval poem that Allan was endeavouring to translate ; and she wanted to know how he was getting on with the laborious task ; and sought to reassure him about his doubts as to whether he should be able to find a publisher. For she was a kindly, helpful sort of creature ; and she had

a resolute faith in the future of this young
man.

The last of the twilight was vanishing as
he parted from them at the house in Camp-
bell-street. And it was with a heavy heart,
it was with a bitter sense of disappointment
and despondency that he turned away and
set out for home. For too surely he had
observed that the first little tentative token
of friendship he had offered to Barbara
Maclean she no longer carried in her hand.
Doubtless she had tossed the worthless thing
aside into the highway, to be trampled in the
mud; or perhaps she had idly dropped it into
one of the brackish pools—half-rain, half sea-
water—out on the dark rocks where they had
been sitting, during an enchanted but hopeless hour.

CHAPTER X.

THE SUN-GOD.

THEN the great evening drew near on which the McAskills of the Argyll Arms were to entertain the members of the Gaelic Choir and other friends; and Peter McFadyen had been as good as his word, he had procured an invitation for Barbara. At first Jess was doubtful as to whether it would be quite fitting for their family, in view of recent events, to be present at any such festivity; but she found that Barbara was not at all sensitive on the point; and the compromise finally suggested by Mrs. Maclean was to the effect that the two girls should go to the soirée and concert, but should either come away, or remain for a little while as mere spectators, when the dancing began. And Jessie was indefatigably kind in looking after Barbara's costume, and lending her

some small trifles in the way of feminine
finery.

"Every one will look at Barbara," said
she, laughing, to her mother, "and no one
will look at me; so it's but right she should
have the choosing of anything I have."

And again Mr. McFadyen was as good
as his word: on the momentous evening in
question, and for mere extravagance and
display, he brought a ' machine ' to take the
two girls round to the Volunteer Drill-Hall;
and Barbara, stepping across the pavement,
found herself ushered into a vehicle the like
of which she had never entered before—a
vehicle with luxuriously-cushioned seats, and
windows that could be shut up against the
rain, and lamps that sent out a soft glow out
into the black night. Mr. McFadyen, fussy,
eager, proud of the charge that had been
bestowed on him—for Mrs. Maclean had
begged to be allowed to remain at home—
was in the highest of spirits; and there were
more triumphs, more feats of prowess, to
announce: Gilmour had again been beaten
on the links that very afternoon.

"It's the Pinnacle," cried Peter, chuckling
and grinning, and he rubbed his hands in
delight. "It's the Pinnacle that bashes

Gilmour every time! And the angry man he is!—smashing at the ball with the lofting-iron, and then grinding his teeth as he watches it come trintle, trintle down the hill again, right back to his feet! Dod, that Pinnacle 'll be the death o' the station-master, as sure's I'm living!"

The way up to the Drill-Hall was along an obscure back-lane; and in the prevailing darkness the 'machine' moved cautiously; but at length it stopped at the foot of some steps in front of a large, oblong building, and Mr. McFadyen descended to hand out his companions. And what was this sound that came from the interior of the hall?—this was no feeble trembling of a Jew's-harp—this was the shrill and warlike scream of the pipes—it was the 'Athole Gathering' that was being played to welcome the now-arriving guests. The proud McFadyen, when they got up to the door, would fain have entered with one of his charges on each arm; but clearly there was no room for this ostentatious parade; and so, as Jessie hung back a little, in her usual fashion, it was Barbara whom he found himself escorting in—Barbara, whose great, beautiful eyes looked with dumb wonder and astonishment

on this gay spectacle—at the brilliant illu-
minations, the walls and ceiling hung with
flags of resplendent colour, the long tables
sumptuously set forth and decorated. She
was bewildered, but not frightened. She
shook hands with her host and hostess without perturbation. And then the three new-
comers moved on to an open space from
which they could the better observe the
subsequent arrivals.

" So you say Allan Henderson is not to
be here to-night," Mr. McFadyen remarked
to Jess. " Why that? Maybe he thinks
his clothes are not quite smart enough for
such a fine gathering."

Jess flushed quickly—perhaps angrily, despite the habitual gentleness of her nature.

"He has no need to think of any such
thing," said she. " He would look well
wherever he went, and in whatever clothes.
It's not clothes that give a man a distinguished appearance."

There was more than a touch of indignation in her tone. And then she went on
again, proudly—

" Perhaps there may be something of more
importance for him to be thinking about
than a concert and a dance in a drill-hall.

Do you know this, Mr. McFadyen—that he
is preparing a lecture on the Folk-Songs of
Germany, and he is translating the lesser-
known amongst them himself? Any one
else would take the Folk-Songs that have
already been translated and be content with
them ; but that is not Allan's way ; he is too
thorough, too much in earnest for that ; and
suppose, now, when the lecture has been
delivered to the Society, it was afterwards
to be put into shape and sent to one of the
great magazines in London—and perhaps
with his name too—that would be something
for one to speak of, and him only a schoolmaster in Duntroone."

"You seem to be very familiar with Allan's
plans," said the town-councillor, rather spite-
fully.

"Then it is not from any boasting on his
part," Jess retorted, with a fine courage.
"It is not boasting that he is given to. And
some day we may not be wondering quite so
much that he found something more important to do than come to a merry-making
of this kind."

"Ay, well, well," said Peter. "Allan is a
good lad. There's many a worse lad than
Allan, whether he has a small salary or a

big one. And I'll buy the magazine, yes,
that I will. I would not be surprised if I
bought six copies of it, and gave them about.
He's a good enough lad is Allan." For he
would not have had this unfortunate little
disagreement continued on so auspicious an
occasion; especially as every moment new
friends were arriving, and he was eager to
show that he had been entrusted with this
guardianship. Which of the younger men
would have been so favoured?

Meanwhile Barbara had not overheard a
single word, so wholly engrossed was she
with the kaleidoscopic and many-coloured
scene before her. But amongst all the
guests who were now assembled there was
one whom her eyes followed with a curiosity
that at length became a species of fascination.
He was a young man of about five-and-
twenty, fair-complexioned, with close-cropped
curly or rather wavy hair of a light golden-
brown. He seemed to be acquainted with
every one; as he went about he was laughing and talking to this one and that; he had
a happy, goodnatured, confident air; he was
much at his ease; his manner seemed to
say that he was pretty sure of his welcome
wherever he went. Then what rendered

him not less conspicuous was that among all the men in the room he alone wore evening dress. Barbara had never seen evening dress before—except, perhaps, as pictured in some stray copy of a penny illustrated paper; but now here, amid these brilliant lights, in this fine company, it appeared to her altogether beautiful. Beautiful was the fine, smooth, black cloth that seemed to show off the young man's figure so elegantly; beautiful the shining shirt-front, with its neat little single stud of gold; necktie and collar and cuffs—all were perfection, and all were worn with such freedom and grace. In dress, in manner, in appearance, he was so wholly different from the others. Could he be the son of some great laird, she asked herself, with a kind of awe. And intently her eyes followed him, as he moved hither and thither, shaking hands with this one, nodding to that—a radiant being—an apparition : had the time come back for the gods to descend and appear among men ?

And then Barbara found herself all trembling—and wishing to be away—and yet powerless to escape. He was clearly coming to this corner; and quickly too; he had a card in his hand.

"How are you, Mr. McFadyen?—I've got you at last," said he, and his voice had a cheerful ring. Then he seemed to recognise the fact that the town-councillor had companions. "Oh, how do you do, Miss Maclean!—I hope you are going to give me a dance to-night—— "

"This is my cousin Barbara, Mr. Ogilvie," said Jess.

He turned towards her with the briefest glance, and bowed. The poor lass—overcome by the splendour of his presence—her eyes abashed and fixed on the ground—made some bungling little effort at a curtsy. It was all she knew; she could do no better; and probably she was hardly aware of what she did. And most likely he did not notice; for he had turned again to McFadyen.

"We've put you down for a toast, Mr. McFadyen," said the young Master of Ceremonies. "You have to propose the ladies—— "

"No, no—na, na," said Peter, in sudden fright. "No speech-making from me—— "

"But why not?—why not?" remonstrated the young man. "You can make fine speeches about water-rates and gas-lamps—I read the reports in the paper every week;

and you're the ladies' man—you're the very
one for this toast——"

The councillor had been disconcerted only
for a moment. He was not going to play
craven, with Jess looking on.

" Well, I'll not deny," said he, pulling
himself up a bit, " that I can say a few
words at a fitting time. I'm not an orator,
perhaps——"

" You'll do just splendid," said the light-
hearted M.C., hurrying away to get his other
business finished—and leaving poor Barbara
with an overwhelming conviction that she
had been guilty of a stupidity and awkward-
ness too dreadful to be recalled or even
thought of.

And a very merry, happy, excited, loquacious assemblage this was that eventually
got itself seated at the long tables ; and
right gallantly did the town-councillor pro-
ceed to look after and entertain his two companions. It is true that at times a thought
of his appointed speech would suddenly
penetrate him ; he would collapse and sink
into himself—no doubt desperately hunting
in the dark spaces of his mind for im-
promptus ; but then again he would rouse
himself and shake off these vain anxieties,

and would strive to convince his neighbours that for wit, and sarcasm, and apposite raillery there was not one of the younger men in Duntroone to come anywhere near him. And Jess was willing to be pleased; it was an animated, inspiriting scene—what with the radiant lights, the festooned flags, the decorated tables; while for variety's sake the general hubbub of conversation would be broken in upon at intervals by the wild skirl of the pipes—the three tartaned heroes marching round the hall playing ' The Hills of Glenorchy,' or ' Hoop her and Gird her,' or ' Mrs. Ronald Graham's Welcome Home.' As for Barbara, she sate as one isolated and estranged. Her eyes followed the sun-god — covertly and intently regarding every smile and glance and gesture. And she had ample opportunity for this secret observation; for the young Master of Ceremonies seemed to be looking after everybody but himself; he went from table to table, joking and laughing, and keeping things moving generally. And Barbara's heart sank within her when she saw that those women he spoke to—maids and matrons alike—were all so splendidly dressed, and had such fine adornments about their sleeves, and their necks, and the doing-up of their hair. She became conscious that her cousin Jess and herself were the two most simply-attired young people in the room—a simplicity that appeared to her a distressing plainness. Had the sun-god taken notice? At least he had not stayed talking to them, as he now stayed talking to those others.

" Jessie," said Barbara, at length—and her eyes were cast down, and she spoke in tremulous hesitation, " who was the—the young gentleman—that came up to you ? "

Jess had forgotten.

" Which one? When? " she asked.

" Before we sate down," continued Barbara. And she ventured to raise her eyes a little. " He is standing over there by the door."

Jess glanced in the direction indicated.

" Oh, that's Johnnie Ogilvie," said she, blithely. " He's the Purser of the *Aros Castle.*"

Barbara was silent for a second or two, gazing furtively the while.

" Does he live in Duntroone ? "

" Well, he'll very soon be living in Duntroone, for they put the *Aros Castle* on again at the beginning of next month. And I suppose that is why he has come through

here to-night—though he is a great friend
of the McAskills whatever." Then Jess
laughed. " But you must not be casting
your eyes that way, Barbara. He's a fearful
lad is Johnnie Ogilvie, for breaking young
girls' hearts. At least so they say. I
do not believe the lad is any worse than
others."

Here silence was called-for by a tumultuous
hammering on the tables that made the
crystal jump, for Mr. McAskill had risen to
say a word of welcome to his guests and to
ask them to drink a glass with him. And
this was the beginning of the speech-making;
but in truth there was not much of it; for
there were many things to be got through.
It ought to be recorded, however, that Mr.
McFadyen acquitted himself well; he was
jocose within due moderation; he paid a
manly tribute to the charms of youth and
beauty; and he earned great applause by
saying he would not detain his audience,
because they were all looking forward to
seeing those bewitching creatures who now
sate expectant by their side—those divine
creatures who were the sweeteners of man's
destiny here below—they were all looking
forward to beholding those angelic forms to

still better advantage in the mazy intricacies of the dance.

Then the members of the Gaelic Choir withdrew and re-assembled on the platform; the remaining visitors also rising from the tables, to allow the attendants to clear the hall. And soon this large, hollow-sounding place was filled with music less ear-splitting than that of the pipes; the sonorous, softened part-singing of the trained choir was an admirable feature of the evening's entertainment; the guests could not have thanked their host in happier fashion. It may be admitted that the majority of these concerted pieces were of a mournful cast; one of them, in especial—'The Braes of Glen-Braon'—in its heart-breaking wail seemed to give expression to all the sadness and loneliness of the remote and sea-swept isles; but those present were familiar with the prevailing character of Highland minstrelsy; they were not too much cast down by those successive 'Farewells' against which Mr. McFadyen had energetically protested. 'Farewell, Farewell to Fuinary!' sang those harmoniously-modulated voices; then came the 'Lament of MacCrimmon'—with one woman's voice ringing clear and high above the low-rumbling refrain, as if it were some wild note heard from the surge of tumultuous waves; they repeated the plaint of the distant lover—

> ' *O could I be, love, in form of sea-gull,*
> *That sails so freely beyond the sea,*
> *I'd visit Islay, for there abiding*
> *Is that sweet kind one I pine to see*'

—with many another favourite. Meanwhile the great hall had been prepared for the dancing; and the pipers were awaiting the word.

"*Suas a' phiob!*" called out the impatient McAskill.

And presently, after a discordant tuning-up of the drones, the pipes broke clear away into ' The Marchioness of Tweeddale's Delight'; and that was the signal for the Choir to come hurrying down from the platform, to secure partners, or to be chosen as partners, for the Grand March was about to take place. Then Mr. McAskill and his sister-in-law led the way; the other couples fell in; the pipers blew their bravest; and down the long hall went the joyous procession, every one elated with thoughts of the gaiety that was about to follow. There had been enough of speech-making and of singing of Farewells; in due course the reel-stage would be arrived at; and the pipers would have encouragement to put fire and glow into the proceedings, if an occasional dram would help.

Now of all the people here gathered together, only three remained apart.

"Really, Mr. McFadyen," said Jess, "I am quite ashamed to be keeping you away from the dancing, and you so fond of it——"

"Not at all—not at all!" protested the gallant Peter. "I undertook a charge, and I must fulfil it. And gladly too. I'm just quite proud and pleased to stay here with you. They'll be plenty of capering later on: five o'clock will not see the last of them out o' this place."

"But if we went away now, it would leave you free," said Jess; and then again, observing that Barbara's attention was so completely absorbed by the pageant taking place before her that it seemed merciless to tear her away, she added: "Well, maybe Barbara would like to stay just a little while yet."

This, at all events, Barbara heard. She turned her great, mystic, appealing eyes to her companions, and said—

"Oh, yes—yes, I would! A little while more, Jessie!"

For it was not only the pageant; better now than before her rapt observation could dwell on the young Master of the Ceremonies, who seemed to combine in himself all the elegancies and graces of youthful manhood—elegancies and graces of a kind she had never hitherto dreamed of. Even his patent-leather boots—the wonderful polish—the pointed and symmetrical shape—the lightness they seemed to lend to his step: this also was another marvel, an allurement, a mystery of fasciuation. And when the Grand March was over and the pipes had ceased, when the band had come on to the platform, and a quadrille was being formed, it appeared to her as though he were the moving spirit in all this brilliant throng : no wonder those finely-dressed dames, and the younger women with their hair done up in fashionable ways, regarded him with favouring looks and answered him with smiling words.

But Jack Ogilvie, Purser of the *Aros Castle*, would have been a very poor Master of Ceremonies had he allowed those three to remain neglected : he swooped down upon them, with urgent remonstrances, until Mr.

McFadyen got a chance of interposing an explanation as to why they were taking no part in the programme. Then the young man went away again, for it was a busy night with him. To Barbara it was as if she had been in a 'dwawm'—a dim, half-conscious swoon—while he was so near her, while the sound of his voice was in her ears.

At length, however, the prudent Jess thought it was time for them to depart; Barbara mutely yielded—with some lingering, backward glances; Peter McFadyen had the 'machine' in waiting; and the girls were driven home under his escort. He left them at the open door—for he was returning to the Drill-Hall, where there might yet be a chance for him to shine in the Varsoviana or the Guaracha; and they entered the house to find the blithe little widow awaiting them, with the inevitable tea-pot on the hob.

" And who, think you," said Mrs. Maclean, as the girls were taking off their things, " who, think you, was here all the evening ? Who but Allan Henderson ! Isn't he the sober, quiet lad to think of coming to talk to an old woman, when you young folks were away gallivanting by yourselves ? Poor

Allan," she continued, as she put the tea-cups
on the table, " I'm afraid he's not very
happy and settled at present. He was
wondering whether he should not try another
country, where there might be a better
opening for him. But we cannot allow that
—we cannot allow that at all! For Allan
to leave Duntroone would be just a public
calumny—— "

" Is it a public calamity you mean,
mother ? " Jess interposed.

" Ay, that's what I said," the widow went
on, in her complacent fashion. " And I was
telling him, instead of going to another
country, he should just start a small boarding-
house in Duntroone, so that some of the
farmers at a distance could send in their
children that they wanted to have regularly
at school. Only, Allan would need to have
a wife to manage for him ; and there's more
than one lass would be willing, that I'm sure
of; for he's a good lad is Allan ; and you're
always saying yourself, Jessie, that he's
astonishing clever, and will do great things
yet. Well well, I hope the struggle will not
bear too hard on him."

Barbara Maclean took no part in this
discussion. She was standing in front of

the fire, staring into it. It was not of the
schoolmaster, and of the poor outlook of his
life, that she was thinking—there were more
luminous, fascinating, wonderful pictures
burning in her brain.

CHAPTER XI.

"THE WILD TEARS FALL."

BARBARA MACLEAN's household duties were light; practically she had the mid-day to herself; and she had got into a habit of stealing out and wandering along to the triple windows of the chief draper's shop in the town, where she would stand gazing with entranced and covetous eyes. This was indeed different from the "merchant's" store at Kilree; here were beautiful kid gloves with furred wrists and many buttons, silk kerchiefs of every hue, ribbons and laces, boas, muffs, tartan scarves, elegant black hats with surmounting black feathers, and a hundred things each more wonderful than the other. And occasionally a waggonette would drive up, bringing in some family of gentlefolk from the neighbouring country;

and as mother and daughters descended, and crossed the pavement, Barbara would watch them with an eager and furtive scrutiny, marking every detail of their deportment and dress. And then she would return to the study of this resplendent finery—which was all so far away from her ; for although her aunt had insisted on her accepting a small salary, it was merely to save the girl's sense of independence, and did not bring these fascinating things any nearer her.

Now by some means or other Allan the schoolmaster had become aware of this trait in Barbara's character, and it greatly interested and pleased him. A man is tolerant and lenient where a woman has thrown the magic glamour of her eyes over him ; this peculiarity, the young schoolmaster said to himself, only proved her to be a daughter of Eve ; she was human, she was one of ourselves ; she was no impossible and visionary maiden come out of the night and the sea. And on a certain afternoon he went along to Jess, whom he found at the counter.

" Jessie," said he, with even more than his usual diffidence, " if your mother is in, could you come with me for a few minutes to McLennan's the draper's ? "

"Oh, yes, indeed!" said the ever-good-natured Jess; but she looked up wondering: what concern could the grave and studious Allan have with a haberdasher's shop?

"I want you to help me to choose a little present—something a young girl would like —something pretty and smart that she could wear—— "

Jessie's face flushed quickly; and she seemed to draw back in confusion.

"But why should you think of such things, Allan?" she said, in a tone of remonstrance. "Why should you wish to give finery to anyone? I know your own tastes are all very simple; and it is not right for you to be spending money in this way—— "

"But, Jessie," he answered her, though still with a certain shyness, "I am anxious that Barbara should feel she was amongst people who wish her well. She is a young girl—and still partly a stranger—and I was thinking if I could get something that would please her—a little present of that kind would at least show a friendly intention—and she would understand it."

He did not notice the swift change of expression—of alarm, almost—that had passed

over Jess Maclean's face the instant he had
mentioned Barbara's name.

"Oh, yes," she said, in eager haste. "You
are quite right, Allan. I am sure it would
please Barbara. And as you say, she may
be feeling a little strange yet in Duntroone.
Oh, yes, for Barbara. It's quite different
with Barbara. And will you be going now?
For I will get ready at once." And with
that she disappeared into the back-parlour, to
fetch her things.

He never knew what keen arrow he had
driven through her heart. For she was a
brave kind of a lass and naturally cheerful;
and by the time these two were walking
along the pavement, on their way to the
draper's, she was making merry over the
idea of the austere and absent-minded student
going to buy millinery, and was teasing him,
and mocking him with her mischievous eyes.
But she was very friendly all the same; and
in the shop her counsel was sage and prudent
—for she knew that, though his means were
scant and his own habits as regarded himself
sparing enough, there was Highland blood
in his veins, and there was no saying but
that he might do something reckless. Eventually they decided upon a *fichu* of black silk,

trimmed with black lace, and adorned with black glass bugles. It was Jess Maclean's inward surmise that the bugles would prove attractive to Barbara.

Then arose the question of presentation; and here again Jess unselfishly came to his aid; she could see that he was awkward and unskilled in such affairs, and perhaps also a little apprehensive.

"Why not come along in the evening?" said she, "and smoke a pipe as usual; and I will send over to the house for Barbara; and you can give her your present without any great formality. Sure I am she will be very proud of it."

"That's what I will do, then, Jessie," said he. "And I am very much obliged to you." And then, having seen her as far as the door of the shop, he turned and made his way home to his books—or to such wild fancies and hopes and fears as would obstinately thrust themselves between him and the printed page.

But he need not have been at all apprehensive as to the manner in which Barbara would receive his present. When, later on, he was in the little parlour, and when, in answer to a message, Barbara came over

from the house, any one could have seen that
she knew what was going to happen: there
was a tinge of pretty embarrassment in her
face, and she shook hands with him in a shy
kind of way, and for a second—O wonder of
wonders!—the beautiful dark-blue eyes, from
under their jet-black lashes, glanced at the
young man with quite unusual and modest
friendliness. He was bewildered—his heart
went beating—so that he could scarce explain
to her his reasons for begging her to accept
this simple gift; but Jess proceeded to open
the small packet; and Mrs. Maclean was loud
in praises of the *fichu*; while Barbara's mystic
and unfathomable eyes were filled with
pleasure when she beheld the silk and the
lace and the glittering beads. Then she
turned to the young man. She hesitated.
And it was in Gaelic that she had to speak
her thanks to him, the English not coming
freely enough or not being expressive enough;
and for another ineffable moment her glance
dwelt upon him with the kindliest regard.
And if he was bewildered before, he was
bereft of his senses now. He had it in mind
to sell his books and all his belongings and
lay out every farthing in McLennan's shop.
But at this point the town-councillor made

his appearance, and something like sanity was restored.

Peter McFadyen, as it turned out, was an angry man. Nay, did not some tone of complaint and reproach run through his tale of injury—seeing that Lauchie the shoemaker was an especial friend of Mrs. Maclean's?

"I just went into the Argyll Arms"—such was his indignant story—"to say to Mrs. McAskill what everybody has been saying ever since the dance, that it was one of the greatest successes ever known in Duntroone; and I was not inside but a few minutes; and when I came out, here was this man Lauchlan MacIntyre—your friend Lauchlan, Mrs. Maclean—and he was waiting for me round the corner. Confound his impudence! 'Oh, Mr. McFadyen,' says he, 'I'm sorry to see ye gang that gate. You've been into the very ante-room of hell. And you a man of poseetion, that should be an example to all of us! But there is time—there is time for you to hold back—you may escape destruction yet. There's a meeting of the Rechabites to-morrow night, and if ye'd come with me, ye might be persuaded to join us. Drink is a terrible thing, but it can be mastered——'"

Mr. McFadyen suddenly broke off.

"Ay, do ye think it is a laughing matter, Miss Jessie?" he demanded—for Jess had been quietly giggling to herself. "That impudent drunken scoundrel!—and me, a town-councillor—and one o' the most temperate men in Duntroone. Find me a more temperate man than I am, in the whole of Duntroone—and I'll eat him!"

"Poor Lauchie!" said the little widow, with easy compassion. "Sometimes I think he is going to keep on the straight road; and maybe he is that way now; but I am never very sanguinary——"

"Sanguine, you mean, mother!"

"Ay, just that. You can never be sure about Lauchie. And it's a bad sign when he takes to the preaching. It's a sign he is likely to break out again. But he's not a bad kind of man, Lauchie: there's many a worse man than Lauchie."

Now the town-councillor, when he had made his protest, and asserted his dignity, had no mind to let Jess Maclean think that he was one to bear ill-will; he dismissed the subject of Long Lauchie altogether; and very soon he was giving his audience, with many chucklings of satisfaction, a description

of how he had that very afternoon triumphed
over all his opponents at throwing the hammer in his backyard. Nevertheless he did
not wholly monopolise the conversation; and
the chubby and chirrupy little man was
sharp-sighted enough; it was not long ere
he perceived that now, when the schoolmaster addressed Barbara Maclean, she turned
to him with a kindly and friendly attention
she had never hitherto paid him. And did
not Jess notice? Ay, and Mrs. Maclean?
As for Peter, he was delighted. If this was
the way things were going, so much the
better for his own daring schemes.

"Dod, man, Allan," said he, as these two
were walking home, through a somewhat
wet and blustering night, " ye're on the track
at last. Ye've made your mark. You'll
have her. She's yours—if you've the courage
to go in and win. I can see it. I'm not
blind. The lass is well-disposed towards ye.
But ye'll have to speak—ye'll have to speak,
man !—— "

"I understand what ye mean, Mr. Mc-
Fadyen," said Henderson, in his grave and
deliberate fashion. "But these are hardly
matters to be guessed at in so light a way.
One must not hope for too much, merely on

account of a little friendliness. And even if
what you say were possible, there are many
perplexities around me and ahead of me. It's
all very well for you that have a fine position,
an assured position, to talk in the heroic
strain; but I have to consider that I might
be dragging into misery, and uncertainty,
and wretchedness, one that's of far more
importance than myself——"

"No, no, man!" returned the sprightly
councillor. "Ye take far too serious a view
of life. Young folk must have courage and
run risks. And if you don't, why, in the
case of a handsome lass like that, somebody
else will be coming along and snapping her
up. Here, Allan, lad," he said, halting—for
they had just arrived at his dwelling-house,
which adjoined his office. "Ye'll just come
in and sit down for a few minutes, for I've
something to say to ye that may be of
importance to ye by-and-bye."

The young man did not refuse. He had
no great love for McFadyen—in fact he was
rather inclined to treat him with impatience
and disdain; but there were momentous
issues at stake; and perhaps some talk with
this older man, who had seen more of the
world, might make matters a little clearer.

So he waited until Peter fumbled in his pockets for his latch-key—both of them no doubt looking forward to a quiet and confidential chat, perhaps with some little solace of tobacco.

There was to be no such thing, at this time and place. McFadyen put the key in the lock, turned it, and was about to enter, when immediately behind the door there was a low and savage growl. He sprang back incontinently, dragging the door to with him.

"Lord's sake alive!" he exclaimed, when he had partly recovered himself. "It's that dog!"

"What dog?"

"The bull-dog I bought from Jamie Nicholson yesterday; and it was to be sent home this afternoon; and that idiot of a servant-lass seems to have left it free in the house instead of tying it up in the backyard. What's to be done? It's a fearfu' beast. Some rascals have been stealing my coals, and I thought I would pay them out——"

"And the dog is strange to you?"

"I never saw it but three minutes yesterday," said the distressed councillor, "and it would not know me from Adam, even if the house was not in darkness!"

Here the schoolmaster broke into one of those portentous guffaws that had so perplexed Jess Maclean ; he roared and laughed ; he better roared and laughed ; while the councillor's temper, amid all his distractions, began to grow warm.

"A man shut out of his house by his own dog ! " Allan cried, with another prodigious fit of laughter. "Well, there's but the one thing for it. Maybe he'll recognise you as the master of the place. Go boldly by him——"

"Go boldly by him yourself!" retorted the councillor angrily.

"But you cannot stand in the street all night ! Where's the maidservant ? "

"She's in her bed long ago ! "

"Well, then, you must go round by the back and get in that way."

"How can I ? What's the use of talking nonsense ? " answered McFadyen, with savage fretfulness. "Do you think I would leave my coal-ree open, when I got this infernal beast for the very purpose o' protecting it ? And the key of the gate's in the office ; there's no way round by the back at all ! "

"Well, then," said Allan, "you'll have to try gentleness. Go in a little bit, and try to humour him——"

"Go in a little bit yourself, if you're so clever!" said the councillor, peevishly.

"What are you going to do? Or will you ask the policeman's advice?—there's sure to be a policeman round by the station."

"I would not allow any policeman to go into that passage—it's as much as his life would be worth!" Peter rejoined in his despair.

"You'll have to send for the man who sold the dog to you."

"Yes!—very likely!—and him at Taynuilt! He went back to Taynuilt yesterday afternoon."

"Very well," said Allan, more seriously, "I'll tell you what we'll do. You cannot stand in front of this house all night. You'll just come along to my room, and you can have my bed, and I'll get a shake-down, or a chair's good enough for me in any case. For you were kind enough, Mr. McFadyen, to hint that there was something you had to say to me; and if it affects what you and I were talking about, I would rather hear of it before going to sleep. It's an anxious time with me. There is not much hospitality I can offer you; but you are welcome."

"Have you plenty of tobacco, Allan?" the

councillor asked, still regarding his own
impossible door.

" Yes, I have that," responded the younger
man. " It's the one thing I can offer you."

" Well and good, then," said he ; but before
he turned away to follow his companion, and
while he was still contemplating the shut
door, he added, bitterly : " You'll see if I
haven't that beast chained up to-morrow, if
there's a blacksmith in Duntroone can fasten
a rivet into a stone wall."

*   *   *   *   *

Meanwhile the two girls and Mrs. Maclean
had shut the shop, and gone over the way,
and partaken of their frugal supper, and
were now enjoying a friendly chat along with
their needlework and knitting. Barbara
was evidently greatly elated over her present, and was more talkative than usual ;
and Jess, who knew not grudging, was
cheerfully responsive. Then the little
widow kept throwing out merry and mysterious hints.

" Ay, indeed, Barbara," said she, as she
was busy with her needle, " ye may well set
yourself up. There may be more in that
present than you're dreaming of yet. For
Allan Henderson has so far paid but little

heed to the young lasses about; and they've
rather been inclined to look asklant at him,
and toss their head, for you know the old
saying : ' *Crone, will you have the king?   I
will not, as he won't have me.*'   And so the
king has thrown the handkerchief at last,
has he ?   Well, well !   And what will they
say now, all them he has passed over ?   Not
a lass in Duntroone good enough for him,
but the minute one comes in from the outer
isles, the misan—the misanthrope comes out
of his cell, and all the world is changed,
and there's a miracle for you !   Well, well,
indeed ! "

And so she went on, and Jess listened in
silence.   For the girl had long ago given up
any secret and wistful hope that Allan might
look her way ; nay, she had argued and
steeled herself into the belief that she ought
to set herself resolutely against any such
thing, even if it were possible.   She had
formed other plans for him : she knew something of his ambitions.   Duntroone was no
place for him.   He was to go away ; he was
to win to the front; he was to conquer
London ; and when he was become a great
man and famous, perhaps he might have a
single backward and friendly thought for

that cousin Jess who had believed in him and urged him on. And in the meantime, and with pride and with a warm sisterly affection she would watch his career.

Apparently this was a very happy evening. But that same night, in the mid-watches, in the darkness, Jess was lying awake. And at such times the nerves are apt to get unstrung and fall away from their ordinary firmness; self-control is not so easy; and certain dreams that she had been ready enough to sacrifice in her auguries of his great future would come back unbidden. Also some lines she had read in an American magazine, that had seemed to her to have in them a curious suggestion of Celtic remoteness, and solitariness, and longing. Why would the Irish girl's song so haunt her brain ?—

" I try to knead and spin, but my life is low the while ;
Oh, I long to be alone, and walk abroad a mile ;
Yet when I walk alone, and think of naught at all,
Why from me that's young should the wild tears fall ?
  .   .   .   .
The cabin door looks down a furze-lighted hill,
And far as Leighlin cross the fields are green and
    still ;
But once I hear a blackbird in Leighlin hedges call,
The foolishness is on me, and the wild tears fall ! "

Well, the 'foolishness' was on her; and she buried her head in the pillow, that was soaked with her tears; and she made desperate efforts to subdue her sobbing. For Barbara was in the other bed; and she would not awaken Barbara with this unavailing grief. Barbara, who was no doubt placidly dreaming of drapers' windows and black glass bugles.

CHAPTER XII.

THE apartment into which the schoolmaster ushered his guest bore evidence of a hard and rigid economy, not to say downright penury. There was no fire in the grate; there was but the one gas jet; the furniture was scant and bare. There were piles of books, to be sure; but they were all work-like volumes; not a gay binding amongst them.

"Now this is what I like to see," said McFadyen, rubbing his hands with satisfaction as he took a seat and looked around. "This is what I like to see. And I know what it means. When I observe a young man that's sober and industrious, and that has got a reasonable salary, when I observe him living pinched and poor, then I know what it means : he's saving up to get married."

"It has not been like that with me, then, Mr. McFadyen," the younger man said, as he produced a small jar of tobacco, the only luxury in the place. "I've had to pay back to my folks at home what they lent me for the classes—and that was the least part of what I owed and owe them. And then I undertook the schooling¹ of my two younger brothers; but one of them has just got a situation, and the other one will soon be looking about too ; so that I may find myself a little freer—— "

" Exactly that ! " said the councillor, cheerfully. "Something freer to tackle the great problem—the choosing yourself a mate. It's what we are all bent on, though some may be a little later than others—— "

" And it will have to be a little later, if ever, with me," rejoined Allan—who was in an unusually confidential mood : he did not often deign to speak of his private affairs. "In my position how could I ask any young girl to take such a risk ? "

" God bless my soul ! " cried the other, "did ye never hear of such a thing as life-insurance ? "

" That is some safeguard for the future, no doubt. But the question is as to the meantime. And if I were to ask any girl to look my way, I should have to tell her my present prospects; and what inducement could I lay before her—— ?"

"Tuts, tuts, tuts, man!" broke in the happy and hopeful Peter. "That's no the way to talk! Do ye think a young lass is to be won over by a parade of gilded furniture? It's not that she has in her mind when her fancy settles on a lad. Na, na. It's not that will tempt her to kilt up her coats o' green satin, like Leezie Lindsay, and be off with him through bush and briar. It's love well won, and the world well lost—that's more like the ticket, man! Prospects? Life-insurance? Is that what you think she has in her mind? Is that what she answers when he asks her the great question? Not a bit. This is more like what her answer'll be—" And here the councillor raised his hand triumphantly, and sang in a brave fashion, and with many trills—

> 'Gang down the burn, Davie, love,
> Down the burn, Davie, love,
> Gang down the burn, Davie, love,
> And I will follow thee!'

Then Peter moderated his enthusiasm.

"Listen to me, Allan. I will not conceal

from ye that I sometimes thought ye had
other intentions, when ye came so much
about the widow's shop. And then again
I said to myself, No, it was only that you
were related to the family, and maybe you
had not too many friends in the town, and
it was but natural ye should foregather with
your own kith and kin. And yet again I
would say to myself, Yes, there's danger:
he's a young man, he has eyes, he cannot
fail to see what a fine creature Jessie
Maclean is—so good-humoured, and clever,
and bright-looking—just one in twenty
thousand——"

"You may say that, Mr. McFadyen,"
observed the young schoolmaster, gravely.
" Ay, or one in fifty thousand."

"But now that I see your thoughts are
turned in another direction," continued the
councillor, "it's a great relief to me; for, to
tell you the truth, I'm not without hopes
that I might get Jessie for myself. That
would be a fine ploy, wouldn't it?—the two
weddings on the same day! And I'll tell
ye what I'll do with ye, Allan, lad, just to
' mak sikker.' Mrs. Maclean says your best
chance is to get married, and start a boarding-
house for scholars sent in from the country.

And that would need some little capital—
the plenishing and what not. Very well;
I'm not a rich man; but I have a bit of a
nest-egg laid by; and I wouldna mind lending you £50, or even £100, to help you at
the start. And I'm sure if there was an
understanding between Jessie and me, she
would not grudge it either. She's a half-
cousin of yours; and you've been great
friends together; I'm sure she would not
object—— "

A quick flush had come over Allan's forehead.

" I thank ye, I thank ye, Mr. McFadyen,"
he said, hastily, and with lowering brows.
" But it is not to be thought of."

And therewith he closed his mouth and
would say no further word about these poor
affairs of his: so that Peter, who was
evidently in a state of buoyant anticipation,
was forced to talk about his own share in
this great project, and to describe those
personal qualifications—physical strength,
skill, tact, knowledge of the world, and the
like—which, as he contended, were fairly
entitled to put the mere question of years
aside. And then, becoming still more sanguine, he grew enthusiastic over the delights

of courtship, and the enchantments of love's young dream.

Now although Allan Henderson had somewhat rudely and abruptly repulsed this friendly offer, it was nevertheless a wonderful thing for him to think of that one or two onlookers had actually been considering the possibility of Barbara's being favourably inclined towards him. All through the uncongenial toil of the next day there ran as it were little flashes of roseate flame; his eyes would become blind to those monotonous forms and their occupants; the grey hours had occasional startling moments when the outside world was revealed to him as in a vivid dream. And when at last it was all over, when he could emerge into the clearer air, instead of returning to his lodging, he struck away on a solitary ramble by sea and shore : there was a lifetime of contingencies to be faced and resolutely examined, so long as that was possible while those quivering, rose-tinted flashes — those fascinating and elusive will-o'-the-wisps — would break in upon his sight and bewilder him.

He left the town by way of the harbour, climbed the Gallows Hill, and proceeded along the edge of the steep cliffs overlooking the sea. The rain of the previous night and morning had long ago ceased; the clouds were now banked up; there was a brooding silence; the click of the oars of a small boat crossing the bay could be distinctly heard, even at this height. And in the prevailing calm of sky and sea and mountain there was something that seemed in a measure to allay the agitation of his mind; there was peace in those great spaces of the universe; a quiet that conduced to a serener and saner contemplation. Wild hopes were dazzling and exciting things, no doubt; but the destruction of them could also be met and endured, by a man.

As it chanced, he had been so profoundly plunged in these meditations that he had followed the coast-line too mechanically, and now he came to the brink of a chasm that struck inland for some little way. He did not think it worth while going round in order to continue his route; instead he sate down on the verge of this deep cavity, letting his legs dangle over; and there he gave himself up to still further wrestling with the problems and distractions that beset him. For one thing, if he were to incur these great responsibilities, he would have to give

up many cherished ambitions—some snatch
of foreign travel—the issue of his version of
the Nibelungenlied—and the like : towards
which he had been hoarding up his savings.
But after all, what were such trivial con-
siderations when compared with the very
crown and joy of life, supposing that were
now to be put within his reach? He could
hardly believe it possible. He had been bewildered out of his calmer judgment by this
sudden friendliness she had shown him during
but one evening. Was it not too much to
hope for that the one creature in the world
whom he longed to have for his life-com-
panion should on her part turn towards him
and choose him out from amongst all others ?
How could such a thing happen? It was
incredible. It was too marvellous a coinci-
dence. Yet what of the marriages of the
people he saw around him? In what pro-
portion of cases—or in every case—had the
man and the woman found each other in this
inscrutable, inexplicable way ?

And so, with his under lip firmly set, his
forehead drawn together, and his eyes
distant, he sate and pondered; until at
length he appeared to make an effort to
throw off this weight of thinking in a

determination to arise and get home : it was
long past the hour for his chief daily meal.
But at this moment, whether it was that his
foot had been resting on some loose stone,
or that his leg had got benumbed, as he
attempted to get up something seemed to
give way beneath him, and the next instant
he found himself slipping down a few inches.
He caught at the nearest object—it was a
small rowan bush—to steady himself; but
the bush came away in his grasp : nay, this
very movement appeared to make his case
worse, and he felt himself helplessly going.
Then he threw himself back, and thrust out
both hands in some desperate endeavour to
grip anything that would check his descent;
he clutched and clung, but all to no purpose,
for the sides of this chasm were almost sheer ;
and the next thing he knew—or half-knew
—was that he was hurtling down into this
black hole—then came a dull crash—a sharp
agony of pain—then silence—and a strange,
not unblissful sinking out of consciousness.

When he came to himself again, stunned
and dazed, he slowly and gradually became
aware of his position. He was at the bottom
of one of those fissures in the conglomerate
rock that abound along this coast, and that

mostly run down to the sea. This one also
trended towards the shore; but there was
no escape for him that way; for the mouth
of the cavern was barred by an enormous
mass of the same rock. However, he was
not much alarmed. He would be able to
scramble up again, somewhere or other. The
sides of the chasm, if they were steep, were
not at all bare; there was a kind of stunted
vegetation—bits of rowan bushes, heather,
birch, and broom—between him and the strip
of daylight; he would choose his upward
path when his head was a little clearer.

Then he essayed to rise; but to his consternation he found himself incapable of
movement, or only of such movement as
caused him indescribable torture. The truth
flashed in on him. Something was broken.
And then for a moment a frantic resolve to
get out of this death-trap possessed him—
at any cost of agony he must win up to the
open again—surely he could drag the broken
limb from point to point, until his fingers
clasped the edge, and he could raise himself
into the blessed freedom of the outer world.
And again and again he tried, making super-
human efforts, and again and again he was
baffled by overmastering pain; until he sank

back exhausted and half-despairing on his narrow bed of withered and sodden fern.

Thus he lay for a while spent and done; but of a sudden something occurred that caused his heart to leap. There was a sound in the road below—the road that shirted the shore; the footfalls drew nearer; he could even in a dull kind of way hear voices— apparently the voices of two men. Surely this meant rescue for him. And when he judged that the men were about opposite to him, he called and shouted; but even as he did so he had a dreadful consciousness that the shouts were muffled—that they did not seem to travel out of this cavern. Nevertheless he continued to call as loudly as he could; until the footfalls gradually ceased; and he was left once more with silence, and the gathering over of the twilight.

He began to reason with himself against unnecessary dismay. He was not much more than two miles from the town. Some children would be sure to come wandering along, if not this evening then on the following morning or afternoon. Or a shepherd's dog would discover him, and its barking would fetch its master to his aid. Or surely, when his friends missed him from his usual haunts, they would organise a search-party. So long as he retained some power of calling to any chance passer-by, he would not abandon himself to despair : whatever might happen, a stout heart could not harm.

Night came early over this deep gap ; and the darkness seemed to last for ever and ever. He listened to the moaning of the wind in the bushes overhead, and to the long-protracted hiss of the waves along the shore. Towards morning—he guessed it must be towards morning, after those immeasurable hours—a few small silver points began to glimmer in the black opening above ; but the starlight was of little use to him except in so far as it showed the skies were clearing. Further hours, as it seemed to him, passed ; and then, with a great rejoicing and re-awakening of hope, he perceived that the dawn was really drawing near. Stealthily, imperceptibly, such strip of the heavens as he could see became of a pearly blue-grey. A little while, and that was more opalescent in tone. Again, a touch of saffron appeared —soft, and distant, and luminous : some bit of slowly-moving vapour looking over to the opening east. Finally the new day declared itself, in a splendour of mottled rose-grey clouds—and he thought of the happy folk in Duntroone.

No, he would not give in. Down here in the cold-hued twilight, amid the livid greens and the wet russet of the bracken, there were thin threads of half-melted snow here and there; and some of these he could reach; and very welcome was the chill moisture to his parched lips. Then again, as the morning wore on, there was the distraction of listening to the occasional faint sounds in the road below; but he had abandoned all hope of aid from that quarter; he knew he could not make himself heard. His only chance was in attracting the attention of some one passing along the summit of the cliffs; and so from time to time, at random, he called aloud, and paused to listen. But hour after hour went by, and no one came near. At times he grew faint. There was an odour from some decayed herb—St. John's-wort, most likely—that seemed to stifle him. Now and again it appeared to him that he was becoming light-headed; the strangest fancies crowded into his brain; he was possessed with a wild desire to shout songs—students' songs: *Gaudeamus—Vive la compaynie—* and even dafter ditties than these— *O*

*tempora! O mores!—Per secale obvenisset,
Corpus corpori.* He had had no food since
the previous morning ; his wild efforts to
drag himself out of this abyss—the agony
he had endured—had left him hopelessly
weak ; and now, with these delirious impulses
and imaginations taking possession of him,
he could only say to himself, "If my senses
go from me, that will indeed be the end."

And thus it was that when, some time
during the afternoon, he saw a head cautiously
protrude itself through the twigs and
withered grass at the top of the chasm, he
did not believe there was anything or anybody there. That was but another of the
fantastic visions that had begun to haunt
him. Nevertheless, he called out as hitherto
he had been calling out at intervals—though
now not so loudly as heretofore, for he was
enfeebled and listless—

"Help ! help !"

The head was instantly withdrawn. But
at the very moment of its withdrawal something convinced him that it was a real human
face that had been cautiously peering down,
and that it was the face of Niall Gorach.

"Niall ! Niall !" he cried, with all his
remaining strength. " Come back ! Come

back, man! Or go and fetch somebody! Tell them! Tell them I cannot move!"

There was no reappearance of that mysterious, peering and prying face; but he comforted himself with the fancy that the frightened Niall had ran away into the town, and that soon succour would be at hand. He waited, listening intently, minute after minute, half-hour after half-hour, hour after hour; and there was no sign. And again the night fell, and the dark.

But this blackness around him was no longer like the blackness of the previous night; it was all filled with light and colour and moving phantasms; there were sounds of music also, some mournful, some gay. Jess Maclean brought him a pitcher of ice-cold water, and he drank and drank, and thanked her, and he did not know why she was crying. Barbara Maclean hung back a little; and he tried to speak to her; but could not. McFadyen came to him with a copy of a great review in his hand; there was an article in it on the new translation of the Nibelungenlied; it was a friendly writing. Again there were students singing in a room in Glasgow—there was a roaring chorus: *The Old Folks at Home* "—then some one sang " *Lieb Vaterland, magst ruhig sein !* "— and this phrase kept repeating itself more and more distantly and softly—*magst ruhig sein*—*magst ruhig sein*—until the lights grew dim—and the apparitions vanished—and there was silence—and oblivion.

CHAPTER XIII.

OUT OF THE DEEPS.

NEXT day about noon Niall Gorach put his head into the little crib of a shop where Long Lauchie was engaged at his cobbling.

"Mr. MacIntyre," said he, in a pleading kind of way, "will ye gie me a piece of leather to make a sooker?"

Lauchie looked up only for a second.

"Away wi' ye, ye idle vagabond!" he said, sullenly. "Better ye would take to some work than come asking for children's playthings. Away wi' ye!"

The half-witted lad had probably expected this rebuff. But he did not go away. On the contrary, with a cautious look round, he advanced a step; and then he said, in a mysterious voice—

"Mr. MacIntyre, if ye'll gie me the piece

of leather, I'll show ye the opening into the Bad Place."

"Ay, ye'll find yourself there soon enough!" said the shoemaker, grimly.

"But I'll show it to ye," continued Niall, with his eyes longingly fixed on the scraps of leather lying about the floor. "And they've got Henderson the schoolmaster there: if ye go near enough, ye'll hear him crying out."

"What's that ye say?" exclaimed the now startled Lauchie—for, like all the rest of Duntroone, he had heard of the inexplicable disappearance of the young schoolmaster. "What's that ye say about Henderson—Allan Henderson, do you mean?"

"Ay, just that," said Niall. "They've got him in the Bad Place, and ye'll hear him crying for help, away down below. And I'll show ye where it is, and there's flames and brimstone, and little devils running about wi' their pitchforks, and the Big Devil, too, and he has fire coming out of his mouth——"

By this time Long Lauchie was on his feet.

"I'm no sure what to believe o' your haverings," he said, and he paused irresolutely, revolving possibilities in his mind.

"Do ye mean to tell me that you actually heard Allan Henderson crying out somewhere?"

"Ay, that I did!" answered Niall eagerly —he saw the 'sooker' coming within reach.

"Where, then?"

"It's a black hole away down past the Gallows Hill. It's the opening into the Bad Place——"

"Come away this minute," said the shoemaker, reaching over for his cap.

"But I'll no go near—I'll no go near!" cried Niall, shrinking back. "There's the Big Devil—and the flames——"

"Ye'll take me to the very spot," said the shoemaker, peremptorily. "And if I find ye've been telling me lies, I'll give ye the finest leathrin' you ever got in your life. And that will be better for you than playing with a sooker."

It was an unlucky threat; for as they set out it was plain that daft Niall followed with the greatest unwillingness: there was a curious, furtive look in his eyes as if he were watching for the first opportunity of escape. But in the meantime Long Lauchlan was a proud man. Had it been reserved for him, then, to discover the missing schoolmaster,

while all the others had been searching about
and telegraphing in vain ? And if that were
so, was it not owing to his shrewdness in
perceiving that there might be some basis of
fact in the murky imaginings of this half-
witted gangrel ? Lauchie saw himself rising
in the esteem of Duntroone, and stepped out
boldly.

And then—for they had to go round by
the railway-station and the quay to get to
the Gallows Hill—his glance happened to
light on the red baize door of the refreshment-room. It was a terrible temptation ;
and instantly all sorts of devil's logic leapt
into his brain. Was not this a great occur-
rence ? Ought he not to fortify himself
against whatever might befall by swallowing
a good, stiff dram ? It is true that his conscience as a Rechabite said No. But what
was this conscience, after all—this unbidden
and unwelcome guest ? His conscience was
only a part of himself; whereas he was the
whole ; and surely the whole is greater than
any part ? ·Why should he be dictated to
by any mere section of himself? Besides,
the whisky of that refreshment-room was a
most superior whisky. And arduous duties
might be demanded of him, if the poor lad

Allan had chanced into trouble. And— and—— Then of a sudden he shut his lips firm and hard ; he kept his eyes straight before him ; and walking stiffly and erect he got safely past the station.

The next moment, however, he awoke to the fact that his companion had vanished. He looked everywhere around ; there was no Niall visible. He could not at all understand this piece of deviltry, until his wandering gaze fell on the bridge they had crossed in coming along—a bridge that here spans a burn, or rather an open ditch ; and it occurred to him that perhaps the young rascal had slipped over the parapet, clambered down, and hidden himself in that unsavoury refuge. He hurried back. He searched hither and thither. At length he saw two elfish eyes peering from under the archway.

"Come out o' that, ye limb o' Satan!" he called angrily. "Come out o' that, will ye?"

Instead there was an instant disappearance. And then the baffled and irate shoemaker began to pick up stones from the road ; and these he endeavoured to shy into that dusky recess. But it was an awkward angle ; most of the missiles struck the bridge ; and at last, seeing there was nothing else for it, Long Lauchie had himself to get over, and scramble down, and make for the twilight of the arch. When at last he had dragged Niall out by the scruff of the neck, and had him up into the open air again, he said—

"That's one leatherin' I owe ye; and maybe there'll be six more before the day's done. Ye imp o' Satan, wi' your witch's tricks! But wait till I get ye home again, I'll give ye something better than a sooker—ay, ay, I'll give ye something better than a sooker!"

And thereafter he drove him on in front, the better to keep an eye on him; and in this wise they climbed the Gallows Hill, and made their way along the summit of the cliffs.

In time Niall began to move more and more reluctantly; he was evidently creeping forward with much apprehension.

"Whereabouts now?" demanded the shoe-maker.

The daft laddie pointed vaguely with his finger.

"Well, go on—go on, man! What are you feared of?" said the gloomy and impatient Lauchie.

"Maybe they'll come out," said Niall, in a whisper, and his eyes were staring ahead. "They hae grippit the schoolmaster, and maybe they'll come out for us. They can run quick, the small ones, though there's no so much flame about them."

"Get on, man, get on!—and let me see the place where ye heard Henderson crying out," said Lauchie; and then he added, in a more persuasive tone, "And maybe there'll no be a leatherin' for ye at all. Maybe I'll make ye a fine big sooker, and when ye've got the string into it, and when ye've soaked it, it will be strong enough to lift a paving stone out o' the street. Think o' that, now!"

But Niall was no longer occupied with playthings. His eyes were full of dread—and his brain was full of cunning.

"Stand still," he said, in the same cautious whisper, "stand still where ye are, and ye'll hear Henderson. The black hole is just along there. Stand still and listen." And as the shoemaker thoughtlessly obeyed—with his own eyes thrown forward—Niall seized the opportunity to dart away from him, flying off with remarkable swiftness.

Long Lauchie uttered an imprecation, and

started in pursuit. But his cramped calling had left him little of a runner; whereas the half-witted creature had the speed of a roe and the agility of a wild-cat. Moreover, he had no intention of making this a race in the open. At a certain point he swerved towards the edge of the cliffs, and suddenly disappeared; and Lauchie, arriving a few moments later, found that he must have boldly attacked the descent, swinging from one leafless bush to another, until he reached the road below. Lauchie, under his breath, called down more curses, and in a morose mood set out to resume his researches alone. He was not quite sure now but that the imp had befooled him from the beginning.

Nevertheless, to satisfy his own mind, he went forward in the direction that Niall Gorach had indicated, spying everywhere about; and in a very brief space he came to the edge of the chasm. At first, in inspecting this deep gap, he could make out hardly anything; but in time, his eyes growing more accustomed, he thought there was some object of unusual blackness lying away down there, at the foot of the narrowing fissure. And the better to examine, he laid himself prone on the heather, just as Niall had done, and pushed his head over the brink: the next moment he was convinced that the huddled black mass down there was human.

"Allan—Allan Henderson—is that you?" he called aloud.

Then he was silent, and awe-stricken. For there was no answer; and it seemed to him that he was in the presence of death. He stealthily retreated from the edge of the chasm, he regained his feet, he set out for Duntroone—something frightened, no doubt, but still considering rapidly in his own mind what ought now to be done.

He had to go round by the railway-station, and about the first person he met was Mr. Gilmour, who promptly offered to send a couple of his men, with a coil of rope. But Lauchie deemed it advisable to go on and tell his tale at the police-station, and there the sergeant on duty at once ordered two of the officers to get ready a stretcher and coverlet. Finally, Lauchie, after a good deal of tracking from house to house, succeeded in discovering the doctor; and the doctor, on hearing the story, immediately went home to provide himself with some splints, cotton wool, bandages, and the like, and also a flask of brandy. Thus equipped,

the little posse comitatus set out, Long
Lauchie being guide. And it ought to be
noted that in these hurryings to and fro the
shoemaker had to pass the red baize door
of the refreshment-room no fewer than four
times, yet not once did he succumb. With
clenched mouth and immovable head he went
resolutely by—human weakness only reveal-
ing itself, after each achievement, in a long,
sad sigh of resignation.

It turned out that one of the railway-
servants had been a sailor; and when they
arrived at the deep cleft in the rock, he
volunteered to descend. And a tedious and
difficult business it was to get this limp and
insensible body hoisted carefully into the
upper air; but at last the hapless young
schoolmaster lay extended on the heather;
and the doctor proceeded to his examination.
The faintest moan now and again was the
only sign of life lingering in that prostrate
form; there was no movement—not even a
twitch of agony as the doctor was passing
his hand over this or that limb, to ascertain
the whereabouts of any fracture: his eyes
were closed as in profoundest sleep.

And meanwhile there were two other
persons who had heard of this discovery and

were now hurrying out from Duntroone. The one was a strongly-built elderly man, whose natural freshness of complexion was for the moment overmastered by a look of vague and anxious alarm; the other, also with apprehension written in every line of her face, was Jess Maclean. They hardly spoke to each other; their thoughts were too intent on what might be awaiting them ahead. And thus they hastened round by the harbour; they ascended the Gallows Hill; they got out on to the bleak and open and undulating moorland. It was a picture of utter desolation: for the afternoon had turned out wild and wet and squally; the livid green waters of the Sound were dark and driven; the heather bent in waves before the blasts of wind; the sea-gulls were calling and screaming in the gusty and lowering skies. But into this picture of loneliness and gloom there came something still more sombre—a small black group of figures who seemed to be carefully carrying some horizontal object. It looked so like a funeral procession that Jess Maclean uttered a piteous little exclamation, and laid a trembling hand on her companion's arm; but this man with the haggard eyes and the now almost bloodless face, did not pause; he went forward, perhaps a little more slowly; and Jess accompanied him, their gaze fixed upon that gradually advancing train.

The doctor had lingered behind, by the side of the chasm, to gather together his surgical appliances, and the station-master had remained with him. None the less, when the men who were bringing along this sad burden arrived at the spot where the new-comers were now standing, they did not wait for orders; instinctively they came to a halt; they guessed that the stranger who was with Jessie Maclean must be the young man's father. And at the first glimpse of the grey and lifeless features, and the hand hanging limp and loose from under the coverlet, a spasm of agony crossed the father's face; he seemed paralysed; he could not step forward, nor did he ask any question; with shaking fingers he reverently removed his hat from his head; and as he did so, he murmured something to himself:

" The Lord gave, and the Lord hath taken away: blessed be the name of the Lord. But it will bear hard on the lad's mother."

It was Jess who came to his aid. She advanced timidly; she took the hand that hung so limply there; and the next moment she gave a slight short cry.

"He lives!—Uncle, he lives!—there is hope for us!" And at this moment the doctor came up. "Doctor," she said, with tears swimming in her eyes, "is there a chance for him?—is there hope for us?"

"Indeed yes, indeed yes," the doctor made answer. "Go on, lads, go on; but gently. Indeed yes," he resumed, turning to Jess. "Lying out for two days and nights in this cold and wet weather is bad enough; and the poor lad has been smashed about sadly; but I know Allan—I know him well—he's as hard as nails when he gives himself fair treatment. And we'll see him through this, or I'm mistaken. There's not so much damage done—a simple fracture of the leg and a sprained foot; but there's the extreme exhaustion, of course. Well, we must hope for the best, Miss Maclean."

"Where are you taking him to now, sir?" Allan's father asked.

"To the poor-house hospital," was the answer. "It's not the best that could be desired; but it's the only hospital we've got."

"His mother will be sore grieved to hear

that," the older man said. "There's never been one of the family near a poor-house; and this one—this one was just the pride of her life."

"It is mainly a question of attendance," observed the doctor. "If you would prefer that your son should be taken to his own lodgings, maybe I could make some arrangement—— "

"Could I be of any use, Doctor?" Jess interposed, diffidently and yet anxiously.

"Would you be willing to help?" he said, at once turning to her.

"Ay, that I would!—that I would!" said she, with an involuntary tremor of the lip.

"Very well—very well," said he; and he stepped on to give the men altered directions.

They were now come to the top of the Gallows Hill, the descent from which had to be managed with the greatest caution. When, at length, they arrived at the foot of the steep incline, the doctor was not surprised to discover that Jessie Maclean was no longer of the company; he thought it but natural she should wish to avoid the publicity of walking through the town with this funeral-like cortège; and assumed that she had gone on ahead to her own home.

He was mistaken. She had gone on ahead, it is true, and with great swiftness ; but it was to Allan Henderson's lodging. And when at last the doctor and his charge arrived, it was clear how busy and alert and dexterous she had been in the interval. Allan's own room was all smartly tidied up ; the gas lit—for the dusk had fallen now ; a coal fire burning briskly in the grate ; the bed carefully made and folded down. Moreover, she had requisitioned the adjacent room, which chanced to be vacant ; and here also the gas was lit ; while a wicker-work easy-chair had been brought in, for the convenience of any nurse who might want to sit up, and read, and listen. The doctor, busy as he was, looked round, and nodded approval.

* * * * *

Later on that evening Long Lauchie the shoemaker and an old crony of his, Donald Crane—that is to say, Donald that worked the crane at the quay, his real name being Donald Macdonald — were seated together in a corner of a favourite howff of theirs ; and Lauchlan was happy. It was the stupidity of the people of Duntroone that seemed to be amusing him most ; he laughed and chuckled to himself; while there were glasses and a pewter measure on the table before him that ought not to have been there.

"Donald," said he, in Gaelic, to the crane-worker—and the crane-worker was a thin little hard man, with a thin hard red face and steel-blue eyes—"Donald, it is you that have some knowledge in your head. But the other people in Duntroone—well, I will give you my opinion about the other people in Duntroone; and it is this—that they were not at home when the sense was shared. To go seeking away along the shore; when the schoolmaster was not a sailor, nor a fisherman, and when it was known he had not taken a boat anywhere: was not that the work of fools? And for a poor idiot lad to get the better of them—well, I am laughing at that, and no mistake! Donald," he went on, suddenly pretending to be sober, "are you not coming up to Fort William with me to-morrow? You will see something: aw, as sure as death you will see something worth while! For I am going to smash the head of the carpenter. I do not want my wife back; and I will not take her back; but it is the head of the carpenter I

am going to smash for him—aw, Dyea, will
not that be a pretty sight!" He laughed
again and again, softly and quietly, in
humorous anticipation; then he made a
grasp at the pewter measure, but found it
empty. " Donald, my noble hero, we will
now have another mutchkin—ay, by the
piper of Moses, we will have another mutchkin—and I will drink your health. Donald,
it is you that are the son of my heart; and
it is you that are coming to Fort William
with me; and we will see if there is not
a drop of Long John left somewhere about
in Lochaber!"

He reached over, and rang the bell; and
a servant-lass appeared. Long Lauchie had
broken out with a vengeance this time.

CHAPTER XIV.

A VISITOR.

So Jess was installed as nurse; and the 'foolishness' was no longer upon her; she was brisk and active and cheerful—especially cheerful when she saw that the care she bestowed on this intractable patient was being rewarded by a steady convalescence. For the young man had naturally a tough and wiry physique, if only he had allowed it a little more nourishment and a little less tobacco; and now there was no tobacco, while there was as much nourishment as was deemed prudent; and the progress made was in every way satisfactory. But intractable he assuredly was. He fretted over the waste of time; he fretted over the expense of certain little delicacies which, as a matter of fact, never cost him a farthing, for they were

sent along out of the kindly thoughtfulness
of Mrs. Maclean; and he fretted over the
rules and regulations that Jess, under the
doctor's orders, had to impose. Nay, to tell
the truth, he was sometimes not over civil to
Jess herself. But she only laughed.

"A grumbling patient is a recovering
patient," she would say to the town-councillor,
who called frequently.

It was not his grumbling that hurt her
and opened old wounds. Oftentimes, when
she went in to sit with him for half-an-hour,
he would talk of nothing but her cousin
Barbara; and the questions he asked showed
clearly enough what was running in his
mind, and what was the future towards
which he was looking. He had got it into
his head that a woman must necessarily
know more of the character, and disposition,
and views of a woman than a man possibly
could; and when he was not himself talking
about Barbara, he would have Jess talk of
her; while Jess, in framing her replies to
his questions, naturally could speak no word
of Barbara that was not hearty commen-
dation.

"And you say she has courage?" he
proceeded, on one occasion. "You imagine

she would not be afraid to face straightened
circumstances ? ''

" As for that," Jess responded, " she has
faced nothing else all her life long ! ''

" Yes, perhaps," he said, after a moment's
hesitation, " but I was thinking if she came
to consider the question of marrying. She
might very fairly look for some better
position—some assurance as to the future :
marriage is a big enough risk in any case,
without any added uncertainty—— ''

" She would have to take her chance like
other folk," said Jess, a little tartly.

But Jess Maclean went and pondered over
these things ; and when in the evening she
took him in his bit of light supper, she
said—

" Now, Allan, you must not keep worrying
about your circumstances and your future, as
I think you do. It is merely that this
accident has driven you to consider possibilities that are never likely to happen. You
are none so ill off, as it is. Mr. McFadyen
has made it all right with the School Board,
and they've got a substitute, and you are to
put aside all anxiety to get about again,
until you are perfectly well and strong.
Then there's another thing. You must give

up the scheme about the boarding-house. It would never do. It would want a great deal of capital; and there would be a great responsibility; and if, as mother suggests, you thought of taking a wife to manage it for you, well, then, how could you go to a girl and say 'Will you become my house-keeper? I will marry you, so that you may look after my boarders?'"

As she spoke thus Jessie's fair and freckled face showed some colour; but she was determined to have her say out; she had more than a casual interest in this young man and his designs.

"Now this is what I would advise you, Allan, if you think it is not too impertinent of me to offer one like you advice on any matter at all. In a town like Duntroone there must be plenty of clever young lads, in the shops and the offices, who have never had any chance of the better kind of schooling, and perhaps some of them half-expecting to have a winter or two at college by-and-bye. Well, now, why not start a Latin class for those lads—from eight till half-past nine in the evening, or from half-past eight till ten? There would be no risk in it; there would be no expense except the rent of a big room, and the gas, and the price of an advertisement in the *Duntroone Times and Telegraph*. They would buy their own grammar-books; and the fees would be all found money to you, once the rent was paid. Now will you consider that, if you must go planning and planning about the future?"

He was immensely grateful. And next morning, when she made her appearance, he said—

"Jessie, you are the wisest creature in the world—and the kindest. I have been lying awake half the night, considering what the advertisement should be, and wondering where I could get a room, and how long it might be before I could begin—— "

"Oh, indeed!" said she. "Well, if it's going to lead to your lying awake at night, I'm not for intermeddling any more in your schemes—or for taking any interest in your affairs. Why should I?" she added, saucily.

"Why should you?" he repeated, with a friendly glance towards her. "Because I don't deserve it. That's the way of women."

And yet it was hard on Jess that she should be deputed to coax and persuade Barbara Maclean into paying him a visit.

For a considerable time he had kept this secret desire of his to himself; perhaps in the hope that Barbara would of her own accord come along to see him; perhaps through some fear that she might be un-favourably impressed by the poor and mean appearance of his dwelling. But the ideas of an invalid are pertinacious; they grow in importance through the long hours of think-ing; and at last, with some little diffidence, he revealed to Jess what he was most of all longing for, and timidly asked her whether she thought such a thing was possible.

For a second Jess remained silent. Then she looked at him rather askance.

"Perhaps," said she, "perhaps you would like Barbara to take my place?"

He seemed startled by the suggestion—but only for a moment.

"No, no," said he, "I could not be so ungrateful. There's no one like you, Jessie; there's no one could be so kind, and forgiving, and good-humoured, in the face of all sorts of unreasonableness, and ill-temper, and ill-treatment——"

"Oh, you treat me well enough, if only you would treat yourself a little better," said Jess, bluntly. "I declare it's most provoking

to see you busying away with your books
and papers and pencil, when it's stories you
should be reading if you must read at all.
I wish your mother were able to come through
to Duntroone, to give you a talking to, for
my scolding is no use—you pay no heed.
Well, I am going along to the house now,
to see if the blanc-mange is ready; and I
will try and get Barbara to come back with
me." And therewith she departed, leaving
him to wait and lie and listen, anxiously and
half-doubtingly and wonderingly, for the first
sound of footsteps on the stairs without.

When Jess had gone along to the house
and got ready the carrageen blanc-mange
for conveyance to her patient, she turned to
Barbara.

"Barbara," she said, "would you not like
to go back with me now, and look in on
Allan, and talk to him for a little while?"

Barbara hardly raised her eyes from her
sewing.

"I am sure that would do no good," said
she, unwillingly. "It would be more of an
annoyance than anything else. And when
he has the doctor, and the landlady, and
you all looking after him, surely that is
enough."

Jess hesitated. She would rather have avoided confessing that it was at Allan's express entreaty she was making this suggestion. But she saw no other way: Barbara was clearly indisposed to go.

"It would be a friendly thing on your part," she said; "for it is very dull for him lying there day after day, and hardly seeing any one. And—and to tell you the truth, Barbara, he asked me to ask you. Come, now!—if it is only for a few minutes."

With evident reluctance the girl put her sewing aside; she got up and fetched her out-of-door things; and presently the two of them had left the house. But they had not gone over a hundred yards when something happened that effectually aroused Barbara from her apathetic acquiescence. There was a distant whistle, repeated again and again— the echo sounding along the shores of Kerrara; and by-and-bye a steamer with flags flying came round the point of the mainland. Jessie's pretty and gentle grey eyes were keen-sighted as well.

"Barbara," said she, "you have been asking me sometimes when Jack Ogilvie was coming back to Duntroone. Well, now, if I am not mistaken, that is the *Aros*

Castle—they are going to put her on her station next week, to Tobermory and Strontian on Loch Sunart. And no doubt Ogilvie is on board of her at this minute."

Barbara suddenly stood stock still.

"Will he be coming ashore? Will he be coming along through the town?" she demanded, hurriedly.

"Very likely," said Jess. "The young man has plenty of friends."

"Jessie," said the other, quickly, "I have forgotten something: I must go back home for a few minutes. Will you come with me, or will you wait here?"

"I will wait here, then," said Jess—for she was at the window of the stationer's shop, and there were plenty of photographs for her to look at.

Then Barbara hastened away back and got to her room; and the first thing she did was to get out from a drawer the handsome *fichu* that Allan Henderson had given her. She whipped off her cloth jacket; she draped herself in that piece of finery; she put on her jacket again, leaving it partly open in front, so that at least a portion of the silk and the lace and the bugles remained visible. Next she went to the mirror, and rapidly and yet carefully attended to her hair, regarding herself from various angles, and slow to be satisfied. From another drawer she took out a pair of kid gloves—whereas when she first set forth her hands had been bare; she provided herself with a silk parasol that she had borrowed on some occasion or another from Mrs. Maclean; she had a final look into the mirror at the set of her hat and its feather; and when she descended into the street, she was quite a smart young lady in appearance. The *Aros Castle* was now lying alongside the quay.

Jessie's quick eyes immediately perceived the change in her cousin's attire; and she said to herself, 'Now, that is a friendly thing to do: Allan will be pleased to see her wearing his present.' And when at length this beautiful creature entered his room, and went forward in rather a perfunctory way to give him her hand, and then retired to a seat a few yards back, the young schoolmaster was not only bewildered and entranced by the mere fact of her being there—by the occasional glance of those large, mystic, deep-blue eyes—he was also overjoyed to see that she wore his gift. He made no doubt it was a piece of kindly thoughtfulness on her part;

it was an indication of the amiability and
sympathy of her nature; it was a token of
goodwill that was worth all the world to
him. He was so grateful to her for coming
—so thrilled and enthralled by the sight of
her—that he did not take particular heed of
her silence, nor yet of the somewhat cold
scrutiny with which she regarded the furniture
of this meagre apartment.

Indeed he was all too anxious to interest
and entertain her; and for that very reason
he found it embarrassingly difficult. Small
talk was not in his way. What he really
longed to say was: 'Do you know how
wonderful and beautiful you are? Do you
know that your sitting in that chair—even
when you are silent—makes a kind of
splendour in this poor room!' But at least
he managed to ask her if she had been to the
recent practisings of the Gaelic Choir, and
whether they had sung the *Fear a bhàta*, or
The Brown-haired Maid, or any other of
the songs familiar in the outer isles; and
this led him on to speak of his lecture on
the German Volkslieder, which had actually
been announced for the 15th of the following month.

"And will you be quite well and going

about by that time?" she asked, turning her great, glorious eyes upon him.

"Oh, yes, and before then, the doctor says," he made answer.

"I am very glad to hear it," she said, rather listlessly—But he did not notice that: the sound of her voice was like music in his ear.

"And I hope you will come to the lecture, Miss Barbara," he went on, presently. "The Committee of the Society have got the loan of the Masonic Hall, that has been all newly decorated—indeed they say now it is the most beautiful hall in all the west country——"

"Oh, then, it is to be a very grand affair?" she said, with a trifle more of attention.

"Well, not such a gay affair as Mr. McAskill's dance," said he, laughing, "that I heard was a great sight for you. But we are to have dignities present. The rank and fashion of Duntroone have been very kind in sending for tickets; and the Committee are trying to persuade the Provost to take the chair. Then I want the front row of seats, next the platform, kept for my own particular friends; I should feel more at home that way; and you and Jessie, if you are so kind as to come, must have seats there—Mr.

McFadyen will look after you—and I shall feel that I am among my own folk—— "

" Allan, lad," said Jess, who was placing a small refection on the little table by the side of the bed, " are you trying to persuade Barbara you are so shy and sensitive before an audience that you need private help and sympathy ? Oh, yes, indeed ! But I know better. I know. I've seen you preside over a meeting, more than once. And I've seen a dispute arise — cross-arguments, confusion, words flying ; and then I've seen the chairman get up, with a face as black as thunder ; and weren't the quarrelsome folk pretty soon quieted down—ordered to the right about, and every one of them feeling he had made a fool of himself ! It is not only in the school that the schoolmaster must lay down the law, and hector, and have everything his own way—— "

" Jessie ! " the young man remonstrated, blushing furiously. " What's this you're saying ? What will Barbara think ? "

" Keep your temper, Allan," Jess responded, coolly. " If ye lost it, it would be a bad thing for the one that found it."

At this point Barbara rose, intimating that it was now time for her to go ; she advanced to the bedside and bade him good-bye; she said a word or two in passing to Jessie; and with that she left.

"There, you see, you've frightened her away with your nonsense!" he exclaimed, fretfully and angrily.

"Better she should go now," Jess said, in her usual placid way, "before she got tired: she is all the more likely to come again."

"And do you think she will come again?" he asked, with a sudden alteration in his tone.

"Why not?" answered Jess, good-naturedly. "She is not kept over busy. I dare say she is away back home now to hem handkerchiefs for herself."

However, Barbara Maclean had not returned home to resume her sewing. When she got outside, she lingered about the pavement, pretending to study the shopwindows, but in reality glancing furtively up and down the thoroughfare, with an occasional look across the bay towards a certain red-funnelled steamer moored at the opposite quay. After a while, and with an affectation of carelessness as though she hardly knew whither she was going, she proceeded along the esplanade in the direction of the railway-station ; and when she reached the railway-station, she went to the bookstall, and seemed to be wholly engrossed in contemplating the periodical literature displayed there. But close to the bookstall there is a large gate-way opening on to the road that here skirts the harbour ; and along this road any one coming either to or from the South Quay must necessarily pass, whether he chooses to look into the railway-station or not. And it was at the South Quay that the *Aros Castle* was now lying.

CHAPTER XV.

Long Lauchlan the shoemaker did not at once put into execution his threat of going to Fort William to smash the head of the carpenter; but the idea remained hidden in the dim recesses of his brain; and one day, having provided himself with a soda-water bottle which was not filled with soda-water, he walked down to the quay, and stepped on board the *Fusilier*. There was no savage purpose visible in his face; on the contrary, he wore an expression of bland content; and when he had gone forward to the bow, and made himself comfortable in a corner, with his back resting against the bulwarks, he was laughing and talking to himself—chuckling over the folly of the contemporary race of mankind—smiling at his own grim little jokes—and occasionally breaking into gentle song. For Lauchie had not as yet returned to the fold of the Rechabites ; the rescue of the schoolmaster had been a great event; and ever since, with but a few intervals of unwilling labour, he had devoted himself to a "terrible keeping-up o' the New Year."

The gangway was withdrawn, the hawsers cast off, the paddles struck the green water into a seething white, and the steamer slowly moved away from the quay. Lauchie was now plaintively singing to himself—

> ' There's nae sorrow there, Jean,
> There's neither cauld nor care, Jean,
> The day's aye fair
> In the Land o' the Leal ! '

"It's a beautiful song—a beautiful, beautiful song," he murmured. Then he burst out laughing. "That foolish idiot of a lass ! ' O Mr. MacIntyre, how dare you mention such a thing to me, and you a married man !' And then says I : ' But a man that has not got a wife is not a married man ; and a man that is not married has as much right to get married as anyone else; and if that is not the law, then it is them that makes the law that have no sense in their head.'" He chuckled again, softly and gleefully. "' O

Mr. MacIntyre, you should not say such things! I am quite frightened to hear you say such things!'" His merriment suddenly ceased. A diligent search had revealed the disastrous fact that in not one of his pockets could a single match be found. And so he was forced to struggle up from that snug corner, and make away for the cabin, where some friendly steward might give him a light for his pipe. And if—as he was in the cabin in any case—and there being a refreshment bar there—if he should take advantage of the opportunity—why——. But Lauchie had disappeared.

When the steamer reached Fort William, he was as blithe and unconcerned as ever; and though he said to himself ' Aw, Dyea, I will make the bandy-legged carpenter dance a little dance!—I will make his bandy legs jump!'—it was said with perfect good humour. And in this happy mood he landed, passed along the quay, and entered the little town that lies at the foot of the great Ben Nevis. He knew that if he were to find the carpenter at all, he would find him alone; for MacKillop was in a very small way of business, ordinarily working as his own journeyman.

At length he turned into an alley, and came upon a yard filled with all sorts of rubbish—old barrels, broken boats, and sodden shavings—at the further end of which was a shed. The shed was empty; and there was no one about. But there was also a workshop; and without a moment's hesitation, Lauchie went over to it, and raised the latch, and opened the door. The next moment the two men were staring at each other—the one in paralysed alarm, the other with a grim sort of humour. Then Lauchie began to look about him for some instrument; and the little, bandy-legged, red-headed carpenter, instantly divining his enemy's purpose, and seeing no way of escape by the door, which was blocked by Lauchie's tall form, made a single spring for the window, and frantically tried to raise the lower sash. But he tugged and shook in vain, for in his haste he had forgotten to undo the catch; and meanwhile Lauchie had got hold of a portentous beam; so that the luckless carpenter, finding himself caught like a trapped rat, could only throw himself under the table at which he had been planing, in some desperate hope of shelter from the imminent blows. And these came quickly enough; and thud after thud resounded of the unequal fray; but what with his laughing, and what with his somewhat unsteady gait, Lauchie's aim was uncertain.

"Aw, Dyea," he called aloud—but without the least apparent animosity—rather with a kind of hilarious enjoyment—" come out of your hole, you red-headed weasel, and I will smash your brains in!"—and therewith he aimed another blow at the carpenter which would undoubtedly have accomplished that object had it not fortunately descended on a crossbar supporting the table. "Come out from your shavings, will you, till I knock your head off your shoulders! Will you come out, now! Do you hear me? Do you think I have come ahl the way to Fort William for nothing? Come away, now! You red-headed weasel, will you come out from your hole?"

And again with a tremendous crash the beam descended—this time, happily, hitting the table itself. Lauchie laughed loudly.

"Aw, Dyea, that a weasel should be afraid to come out like that! Will I get the dogs and worry you out? But no—no, no!—you red-haired son of the devil, I will reach you yet, if I have to keep hammering ahl the day long."

Then something tumultuous, amazing, inconceivable happened. Lauchie vaguely knew that the carpenter had darted out from his retreat and hurled himself against his (Lauchie's) legs; there was a wild scuffle and scramble; the carpenter managed to regain his feet and make for the door; and when the injured husband, seeking to pursue him and belabour him, would have followed, he, that is to say, Lauchlan MacIntyre, tripped over a plank of wood, he lurched heavily forward, he came down like a log, and there was a splintering crash of glass that told of an appalling and irremediable catastrophe.

For a time Lauchie lay motionless, while the peccant carpenter was fleeing away into safety. And when he slowly rose, there could be no doubt as to the calamity that had occurred; his nether garments were saturated; a pocket of his coat was filled with broken glass. More in sorrow than in anger, he pulled out these fragments of the soda-water bottle, and dropped them in the yard; then with an ever-increasing dejection he made his way along the chief thoroughfare in the direction of the quay; and it was a perfectly heart-broken man that seated himself on an empty herring-barrel, to await the return of the steamer from Corpach.

When Lauchlan stepped on board the *Fusilier*, on her homeward voyage, he looked neither to the right nor to the left, but went away forward and sate down, his naturally dismal countenance now heavy with gloom. It was at this moment that a little man dressed all in Sunday black, and with a tall hat on his head, came up to him and said, sympathetically—

"How are ye, Mr. MacIntyre? I'm afraid ye look rather down in the mouth."

"I've had a sad loss, Mr. Robertson," answered Lauchie—but he paid little heed to the Free Kirk elder, who was returning from Achnasheen, where he had been engaged with others in protesting against the Declaratory Act.

"So I have heard—so I have heard," said the elder, with compassion: he knew the story of Lauchie's domestic misfortunes.

"The best Glenlennan," Lauchie murmured to himself.

"Do ye say that now?" rejoined the other. "The best in all the glen, was she? It's grievous to think how time changes us poor mortal creatures ! ”

“ Seven years in bond,” continued the doleful shoemaker.

“ Indeed, indeed ! ” said the elder, shaking his head sadly. “ Seven years in the bonds of iniquity. I had little idea there were such goings-on, over so long a time.”

“ But there was no help for it—no help,” Lauchie murmured again, talking to himself mostly, with his eyes bent on the deck. “ It was bound to happen the moment I fell.”

The elder started.

“ You fell likewise ? ” he exclaimed, in an awestricken voice. “ Dear, dear, that ye should have to tell me that ! But the heart of man is deceitful above all things, and desperately wicked.”

“ Nothing left but bits o' glass—and all the fine stuff gone. There was nearly a whole mutchkin. I was saving it up for the trip home. Seven years’ old Glen-lennan ! ”

The elder stared at him, partly in amazement, partly in anger.

“ Mr. MacIntyre, are ye in your senses ? In the name of mercy what are ye talking about ? ”

" Seven years' old Glenlennan," Lauchie repeated, mournfully. " And when I fell the bottle went all to splinters."

" Ay, the bottle," replied the other, sharply. " I'm thinking ye've been paying too much attention to the bottle of late. And you that was a Rechabite—— "

" And I am a Rechabite. From this moment I am a Rechabite," continued Lauchlan, doggedly. " As sure as death, Mr. Robertson. I'm determined this time. From this moment, not a drop. You'll see— you'll see. And on the strength of it, now, we'll just go down below and have a tasting—— "

" Me ?" said the elder. " Me, that has an example to set—unworthy as I am—— "

" Then I draw back," interposed Lauchie, with decision. And he went on, assuming a certain solemnity of air : " And who will be responsible for that ? Who but yourself, Mr. Robertson ? It is you that have refused to pluck a brand from the burning."

The argument was irresistible. Together they went down to the cabin to celebrate and confirm the most recent of Lauchie's many conversions; and as the story of Allan Henderson's mishap and rescue had to be

told all over again, they were still sitting
in the cabin when the *Fusilier* arrived at
Duntroone.

———

One day at this time, Barbara Maclean was
seated at the window of her room, sewing,
with an occasional glance into the street
below, when she saw Jack Ogilvie pass along
the other side of the thoroughfare. It was
a chance she had been looking forward to,
perhaps watching for; immediately she rose,
threw aside her work, and began with great
rapidity to array herself in such out-of-door
finery as she possessed, not forgetting to lay
her cousin Jessie's stock under contribution.
For hitherto she had been unsuccessful in
obtaining even a few words of speech with
the all too handsome Purser, who had
bewildered her senses away on the evening
of Mrs. McAskill's dance. Once or twice she
had wandered round in the direction of the
South Quay; and she had actually in the
distance seen Ogilvie—smarter than ever in
his uniform of navy blue and brass buttons—
standing by the gangway of the *Aros Castle*,
superintending the embarkation of passengers;
but she had not had the courage to go nearer.
Perhaps he had forgotten that he had ever

met her. He might not even know her name. He had to encounter so many people in the course of his duties.

But now that he had gone along this Campbell Street alone, and would probably return the same way, he might possibly recognise her as he passed. Accordingly, as soon as she had *fichu*, jacket, hat, gloves, and parasol complete, she stole downstairs, and went out on to the pavement. Of course, she could not remain here; for her aunt's shop was just opposite; and Mrs. Maclean might happen to look out, and espy her, and wonder what she was doing. But a short way along there was a watchmaker's window into which she had been in the habit of staring ever since she came to Duntroone; for in it was an ingenious little clock the time of which was kept or rather marked by a tiny gold ball that rolled down an inclined plane, the plane reversing itself at the end of every quarter of a minute; and this toy had fascinated her so that she would stand unweariedly following the zig-zag course of the small gold sphere. It was in front of this window that she now lingered, her eyes peeping corner-wise. And before long she became conscious that someone was approaching;

a furtive glance assured her that this was indeed none other than Ogilvie; and so, with apparent carelessness forsaking the toy-clock, she continued on her way, as if she were not expecting to meet anyone.

It was a quick, light, elate step that now sounded along the pavement: she made certain that in his youthful and joyous audacity and unconcern he would not recollect her or even look her way. As he approached, her heart beat wildly; her trembling fingers grasped the handle of her parasol as if for support. He drew nearer—she could not raise her eyes—he would go by without a word or a glance. And as a matter of fact he did pass her; then almost at the same moment he seemed to pause; she managed to turn her head the least little bit; and forthwith he came forward to her, in a manner doubtingly, yet with a propitiatory smile.

"Miss Maclean?" said he, and he raised his cap and held out his hand. "I beg your pardon—I was nearly being very rude—but you remained so short a time the night of Mrs. McAskill's dance. And how is your cousin, Miss Jessie?" he went on—for he could see that she was overwhelmingly embarrassed and self-conscious; and he was a good-natured lad; and the spectacle of beauty in distress aroused his sympathy. " I heard from her the other day—about the lecture in the Masonic Hall—Allan Henderson the schoolmaster is a great friend of hers and her mother's, and they are anxious he should have a good audience."

" And are you going to the lecture ?" said Barbara, finding her voice at last, and even succeeding in letting her eyes question him for a moment.

" Well, I am not so sure," he made answer. " It is not much in my line; but if the boat is in in good time, I may go. And I will take one or two tickets whatever."

Now at this point he ought to have said good-bye, and gone away. But she was a remarkably pretty girl.

" I hope, Miss Maclean," said he, " that the next time you come to any such gathering, you will stay and join in the dancing. It was quite a disappointment to many of us that you and your cousin left so early. And I suppose you are as fond of dancing as most other young ladies."

" There was not much dancing in Kilree," said Barbara, blushing furiously.

And then at last he did say good-bye, and raised his cap, and departed; and Campbell Street—though it was high noon—seemed to her to grow dark.

No sooner was he gone than she hurried back to her room, and there she went straight to the mirror, to examine her appearance and her costume from every possible point of view. And then, taking off some of her things, she sate down and pondered—until it was time for her to see about getting ready the mid-day meal.

In the afternoon she was once more alone —that is to say, she was free to leave the house in charge of the girl Christina; and again she wandered out, this time making by a circuitous way for a certain back street. Arrived there, she stopped in front of an entry where a small brass plate informed the public that 'Professor Sylvester, teacher of dancing and calisthenics' abode within; she hesitated for a second or so; then, summoning up courage, she passed into the dark entry, rang a bell, and inquired if Professor Sylvester were at home. The next thing was that she found herself the sole occupant of a large and empty apartment, almost destitute of furniture save for a bench that

went along two of the walls, and a table on
which were ranged a number of stone ginger-
beer bottles and tumblers.

The door opened, and the professor appeared, violin in hand. He was an elderly,
spare, careworn-looking man ; his demeanour
was submissive and deprecatory ; he spoke
with a slightly foreign accent when he
addressed her. And his terms, when Barbara
timidly asked for them, were of the most
modest character.

" But I must see where you will begin—I
must see what lessons you will need before
joining the class," he said. " And I will call
in my daughter to be your partner."

He rang the bell. A sandy-haired and
rather sulky-looking girl appeared, who,
recognising the situation at a glance, took
down from a peg on the door a sailor's jacket,
and this she donned, no doubt intimating
that she had now become a male partner, and
was ready, in an impassive and perfunctory
way, to go through her share of the performance. Barbara betrayed the greatest
shame and confusion.

" No," said she, " I cannot dance at all. I
must begin at the beginning. And could
I have lessons without any one looking on ? "

"Certainly—certainly," said the grave and worn-eyed professor. "And what time of the day would it please you to come?—for there are generally some young people here in the evening."

There was no difficulty about making final arrangements; and when these were completed, Barbara, leaving the dancing-master's house, returned home by a roundabout route, for she had resolved upon keeping this matter a dark secret from her aunt and her cousin. And so apt and assiduous did she prove to be that in less than ten days' time the professor said to his daughter—

"Eugénie, I do not think in all my life I have known a pupil like that—so quick, so clever, so graceful in every movement. It all comes naturally to her—no effort—no constraint—it is a pleasure to teach her. If she had been trained from infancy she might have had a career."

Eugénie the sulky did not respond. She had formed an unreasoning dislike towards the new pupil—perhaps through jealousy of her elegant figure and her all-conquering and pathetic eyes.

CHAPTER XVI.

THAT was a great occasion when the young
schoolmaster, though still something of a
cripple, made his first reappearance in Mrs.
Maclean's back parlour. The kind-hearted
little widow, with covert tears in her lashes,
did not know how to tend him and pet him
enough; would have him sit in her own
armchair; feared he was too near the fire,
or too far away from the fire; and generally
made such a fuss over him that he had
shamefacedly to protest again and again,
for he did not like being treated as a child
before Jess.

"Well, indeed," said the widow, as she
brought out currant-bun, shortbread, and
other elements of festivity, "when something
terrible bad has happened, they proclaim a

day of general mutilation throughout the country——"

"Humiliation you mean, mother," Jess said, impatiently—she did not mind at other times, but when Allan was present these harmless little mistakes vexed her.

"Exactly that," continued the widow, with much content. "And when something terrible fine happens, like Allan here getting about again, there should be a general rejoicing among us, if one could only manage it. But in the meantime, Jessie, you'll just step across the way and bid Barbara smarten herself up, and come over, directly. Oh, well I know what pleases young folk! When a lad and a lass are thinking of each other, it's little else they think of. Give them a look at each other, and that's enough—so off ye go, Jess."

Despite herself, a shade of mortification passed over Jess Maclean's face when she was thus ordered to go and summon Barbara; for in her capacity of nurse she had established a sort of proprietary right in this fractious invalid; and now that he had come to report himself convalescent, she thought it hard that any half-stranger should be allowed to intervene. But she was a biddable lass;

she whipped on her shawl and bonnet, and
went away to execute her mission; the only
thing was that on her return she did not
accompany Barbara into the parlour. She
remained in the front shop. And at the
same moment—whether out of mischief or
out of sympathetic consideration — Mrs.
Maclean made some excuse and joined her
daughter; so that Barbara Maclean and the
young schoolmaster found themselves alone
together in the hushed little room.

"It is I that am pleased to see you going
about again," she said in Gaelic, and she
gave him her hand for a moment, and then
composedly took a seat.

"And surely," said he in the same tongue,
" my first visit was due to the house that has
been so kind to me."

He had paled slightly on her entrance;
but now the joy of actually beholding her
had recalled something of colour and animation to his face; his dark and glowing eyes
drank their fill of her, and yet were never
satisfied. How beautiful she was—so much
more beautiful than the phantom image of
her that had occupied his waking dreams;
his covetous longing to secure this glorious
creature all to himself seemed to run riot in

mad fancies; something appeared to whisper
to him that, now when at last she was so
near him, he must seize her hands, and hold
them tight, and say to her ' You are mine—
you are mine—you cannot go away from
me—not any more, for ever.' Meanwhile
Barbara was twiddling with the lace frills
of her cuffs.

"And you," he continued—getting some
mastery over himself, and dismissing these
delirious imaginings, "You I am sure have
found the house a kind house, with a warm
hearth for you."

"Oh, yes, indeed," replied Barbara, rather
indifferently.

"The night of the wreck of the *Sanda*,"
he went on—his glowing eyes still dwelling
on her—his nostrils sensitive to the scent
of her costume—"I thought you were lonely
and sad enough; but I told you you were
going to a friendly home, and I knew that
a friendly home you would find it. And
who but I was the first one to meet you?—
so that ever since I have thought of you, and
been anxious to know that you were well
looked after; and not like one strayed into
a strange fold. Many is the time I would
like to have sent along to ask you to come

and see me, that you might talk about
yourself; but I was not so bold, to disturb
you. But I often heard of you; and I was
sure that from your aunt and your cousin you
would have the kindest of treatment—— "

"Indeed I have nothing to complain of,"
Barbara said—with a glance towards the
glass door : perhaps she was surprised that
she was being left alone in this fashion.

"When a man lies sick in bed he has time
to think of many things," the schoolmaster
proceeded—not quite knowing how to make
use of these invaluable moments—having so
much to say, and yet in a bewilderment of
hesitation as to how far he dared go—"and
above all things I was anxious you should
understand and be sure that you were among
people who wished you well. And perhaps,
here or there, might be one whose interest in
you was warmer than that—if the time was
come to speak——"

Perhaps she comprehended his meaning ;
perhaps not; at all events she somewhat
abruptly rose, and said—

"I am wondering what my aunt is about,
and Jessie : it is not usual for them to
neglect you in this way."

And with that she went to the windowed

door, and opened it, and looked into the
front shop. But at this moment the arrival
of a new visitor—a stormy visitor—absorbed
attention : it was the town-councillor, who
had come hastily along on hearing of Allan's
having adventured forth ; and now he was
all excitement and importance in his desire
to dominate such a situation ; he drove the
Macleans before him into the parlour—the
door being left a bit open as was customary.

"Man, Allan," he cried. "I'm just delighted to see ye here again, among your
own kith and kin, and in a cosy circle too.
And I've news for ye, lad, I've news for ye ;
if ye'll not think I have been taking too
great a liberty ; but I hardly expected to see
ye about so soon, and so I have been making
inquiries on your behalf. Yes, indeed,"
continued Mr. McFadyen, with great vivacity
—regarding himself as the hero of the hour,
no doubt, and conscious that Jess Maclean's
eyes were upon him—"the moment Miss
Jessie put that idea of the Latin class into
my head says I to myself, 'Well, if Allan
is laid by the heels, and cannot look after
this matter, it's just me that's going to do
it for him.' And I've found a splendid
room for ye—the very ticket : the top floor

at Ross and Maclagan's, the lawyers; and
I'm sure they'll be reasonable about it, for
it's empty, and not a bit of use to them.
And just as I was thinking it would cost ye
a stiff penny to put benches and desks into it,
then I chanced to hear of the Masonic Hall
folk wanting to sell off a lot of their old
chairs, and says I to myself, 'If we can get
them cheap, they'll just do fine.' Then I
went to the office of the *Times and Telegraph*,
and saw the manager, and he says if ye'll
give him the advertisement by the year, he'll
take it on the easiest terms; in fact, he was
hinting it might not cost ye anything if you
would do some writing for the paper at odd
hours——"

"No, no," said Allan, frowning, "I will
not have it that way."

But Peter McFadyen was not the man to
be daunted.

"Just as ye like—just as ye like," he said,
blithely. "And that's not all the news.
For I've been asking a question here and
there, I hope in a discreet kind of way, and I
find there's several of my own friends would
like their boys to get an hour or two's Latin
after the office-work or the shop-work was
over; and that's how it stands, Allan, my

lad, that as soon as you care to start, I'll
guarantee ye'll have quite a respectable size
of a class within a fortnight; and there's no
reason why such a class should not go on
growing bigger and bigger, for I find it is
greatly wanted in Duntroone."

"I am sure I am very much obliged to you,
Mr. McFadyen," the young schoolmaster said,
" and especially to Miss Jessie, for it was she
that first thought of it. It's a good thing to
have friends."

He ventured to glance towards Barbara.
Was she betraying any interest in these poor
schemes of his? Nay, could he dare to hope
that she was personally concerned in them?
But Barbara was staring into the fire, with
abstracted gaze.

The councillor, who evidently regarded
himself as the founder of Allan's fortunes,
now proceeded to prophesy great things; and
he was in a humorous mood as well; those
were gay pictures he drew of the future.
Even the little widow was constrained to
remark—

"Well, Mr. McFadyen, it's you that are in
high spirits the night. But take care. Do
you remember the old saying ' *You are too
merry, you'll have to marry.*'"

The warning only increased the councillor's jocosity.

"Faith, that's a good one!" he cried, with a prodigious laugh. "Me marrying? Is that your advice, Mrs. Maclean? That's a fine idea, to be sure—the idea of me marrying!"

"I do not see what there is to laugh at!" the widow protested.

"Well, then, I'll tell you what stands in the way," he said, with sudden gravity—but it was only part of his profound facetiousness. "There's one very good reason, and one's enough; and the reason is that I'm too bashful. Ay, there it is—that's the truth."

With beaming face and demurely twinkling eyes he glanced from one to the other: to himself the notion of his being bashful—a man of the world like himself being bashful —was irresistibly comic.

"I do not know about that," said the downright little widow; "but when I was young, if a man had made up his mind about the girl he wanted to marry, I'm thinking there was not much difficulty about his finding words to ask her. Maybe it is different nowadays. Nowadays it seems to be money first, and your sweetheart second.

Here have you yourself, Mr. McFadyen, been planning out all that Allan is to be, and the grand things he is to do; and yet never a word about his taking a wife—though perhaps there would be no great need for him to go far afield."

These words were spoken with smiling significance—the widow being clearly proud of her diplomacy; but nothing short of consternation ensued. Jessie looked particularly distressed; Barbara betrayed less confusion—indeed she appeared to treat this open innuendo as of little import. As for the young man who had thus been almost invited to choose one of the cousins, he maintained a stern silence. It was the councillor who came to the general relief.

"If there's one thing in the world I would like," he said, "it's just this—that the five of us that are here at this moment could get away for a trip to London to see the sights. Wouldn't that be worth while?—just by ourselves—a little party—and I've been to London myself—— I know my ways about —I could show ye all the fine things that belong to the nation, and therefore they belong just as much to you or to me as to anybody else."

" Indeed there's truth in what ye say, Mr. McFadyen," the schoolmaster put in. " And maybe John Smith—the common man, the poor man—would be a little better contented with his lot if he only remembered what great possessions are his, and what has been done to please him. If John Smith were a philosopher, he would begin and ask questions. For whose delight, for whose use, are splendid public buildings built, and bridges thrown across rivers, and handsome embankments made ? These belong to him—the poor man —to John Smith. What Prince or Duke has a collection of pictures like the National Gallery ?—that is John Smith's. The gems and antiquities and books of the British Museum, the art treasures at South Kensington—what private collection has anything to compare with them ?—and they all belong to John Smith, who has no trouble about them, no fear of being swindled, the best experts of the world buying for him everywhere. The Queen has a fine garden behind Buckingham Palace ; but it's not a third as big as Hyde Park—which is John Smith's domain. For I've been to London too, Mr. McFadyen," continued the schoolmaster, who could talk freely and spiritedly enough when his sombre fits of silence were abandoned, "and I've seen the Green Park, Regent's Park, Battersea Park, and the rest of them, and their ornamental waters, and their great staff of gardeners—all kept up for the public use. What Duke or Marquis has a hall to compare with Westminster Hall—where plain John Smith can walk up and down at any time of the day and eat an orange in contentment? Royal Processions to St. Paul's—Lord Mayor's Shows—pageants of that kind are designed for the poor man, not the rich. And if we here, Mr. Councillor, should ever go to London together, and when you'll be taking us to the British Museum or to South Kensington, you'll just have to drop a word now and again reminding us that these are our own collections, and better than any other in the land, and kept up for us with the greatest care. I wonder now," he said, turning to Mrs. Maclean, " I wonder, when Mr. McFadyen goes with us to the National Gallery, if he'll remember his position. Will he take us up to the famous Raphael, and say to us : ' This is my last great acquisition : I had to pay a little trifle of £70,000 before I could get it away from Blenheim Palace.' "

The practical little widow was puzzled by

these vagaries: her answer was more to the point.

"So you would be off to London, the lot of you?" she said, cheerfully enough. "Well, well, that's natural for young folk; but such gaddings about are no for an old body like me. I'm tied to the premises; I'm a fixture here as much as a shelf or a gasalier—— "

"Not at all—we'll not stir without ye," Peter insisted, gallantly. "Not one step will we stir. You'll just have to get somebody ye can trust to take your place in the shop; then off we go—like school-children for a holiday. It's but right—it's but right, Mrs. Maclean. Year after year we keep on working and working: are we never to give ourselves a bit treat? I'll undertake to say there's not one in this room has seen the Queen. But we've a right to see her; for she's a part of the Constitution that we pay for. Dod, man, Allan, ye put bold ideas into folks' heads; for if everything belongs to John Smith, and if I am John Smith—as ye plainly intimate—then I am the richest man in Europe; and surely the richest man in Europe should be able to afford a trip to London. What d'ye say, Mrs. Maclean?

And you're coming with us, mind. Not a foot will we stir without ye. My word, we'll make things lively in the big town!"

But it was not until Mr. McFadyen and Allan had left the hospitable little parlour, and started off for home, that the councillor revealed the secret reason for his thus insisting on a quite chimerical project.

" Did ye see how I managed it?" he said, with great exultation. " Did ye see how natural-like I led them on to look on us all as forming a family-party—that's you and Barbara, and me and Jessie, with the old lady as general friend and adviser. For it doesna do to frighten them at first. It's like taming a wild animal—ye must be cautious and slow and cunning. Dod, man," exclaimed the councillor, honestly, " I think I showed a little skill! Did I not, now?—did I not?"

Allan was silent: his thoughts were elsewhere. But Mr. McFadyen was not to be discouraged.

" What care I," he continued, gleefully, " whether such a trip as that to London is impracticable or no? Jessie and Barbara have been led into thinking of the four of us being there together, with perhaps the old lady left behind in Duntroone. And of course that would mean two weddings—two weddings, you rascal!—and when the two weddings come about, you'll just tell me if I did not show a little tact and address in paving the way and making everything easy."

"I do not like the sound of the wind," said Allan, absently staring out towards the moaning and inscrutable sea. "It is going to be a wild night."

"Ye're a clever chiel, Allan," continued the complacent councillor, as the two men paused for a second at the parting of their ways, "and your head is just filled with learning and knowledge. But it takes experience of the world, it takes experience of human nature, to manage a difficult affair like this; and maybe you'll be the first to acknowledge as much—maybe you'll be ready to confess that much—when you and Barbara and Jessie and myself find ourselves in a carriage together, driving about and seeing the sights of London."

The schoolmaster did not reply. With a brief "Good-night!" he turned away—and disappeared into the darkness.

CHAPTER XVII.

A PTARMIGAN BROOCH.

It was indeed a wild night — the wind howling in the chimneys and shaking the windows, the rain falling in torrents, the long swish of the waves heard all along the shore; but towards morning there came a sudden and unaccountable calm; and daybreak revealed a brooding stillness over land and sea—revealed a slate-hued world, vague, and dull, and sombre, with the mountains of Mull and Morven hidden behind a dark, formless, impenetrable wall of vapour. Nevertheless, sullen as the outlook might be, there was steady progress towards the light. Up in the high portals of the east, a curious kind of glare began to elbow its way through the heavy masses of cloud; the slopes of Kerrara answered in warm tones of saffron and orange and golden-green ; as the hours went by, the heavens became more and more broken up ; by noon there were shafts of sunlight here and there, and a vivid and welcome blue in the far stretches of water outside the bay ; while the Mull and Morven hills were gradually returning into the visible universe, after their sojourn in unknown space.

And perhaps it was merely this unexpected clearing-up of the morning that drew Barbara Maclean away from her household duties ; but at all events, before going out, she dressed herself with unusual care, for the better display of such small articles of finery as she possessed. When eventually she left the house, she took her way along the sea front, apparently with no very set purpose. She passed the railway-station. She reached the South Quay, at which the *Aros Castle* was lying ; but, as a single swift and covert glance assured her, no officer was visible on board ; it was not yet time for the steamer to sail, and at present the only work going forward was the trundling-in of barrow-loads of coal from the adjoining trucks. She continued her seemingly aimless stroll. She arrived at the foot of the Gallows Hill ; and here she lingered about for some little time. looking at the nets and boats and white-washed cottages that are a survival from the time when Duntroone was little more than a fishing village. The sunlight was becoming more and more general. There was a spring-like mildness and sweetness in the air. The waters of the bay were now a shining azure as well as the further plain; and the long spur of Kerrara shooting out into them, was of burning gold.

And when she turned to make her way back again, she was regarding an equally cheerful scene—the wooded hills, the houses dotted on the slopes, the ivied castle at the point, the ethereal mountains of Morven beyond the blue; and it was but natural that when she came to the coal-trucks, she should go outside, otherwise her view would have been debarred. But passing outside the coal-trucks brought her close to the *Aros Castle* —indeed, she had to go by within touching distance of the gangway; and it was at this moment that she chanced to raise her eyes— and behold! here was the Purser, talking to a friend. He immediately turned from his companion, and addressed her as she approached.

" Are you going a trip with us to-day,
Miss Maclean ? "

" Oh, no," she answered, in pretty confusion ; " I—I only went to have a look at
the old part of the town."

" Then if you will come on board," said
he, politely, " we will take you across to
the North Quay, and it will save you the
walk round. We are off in a few minutes
now."

" Oh, thank you indeed," said she, with
modest and smiling eyes ; and forthwith she
passed along the gangway, he following ;
and she stepped on to the upper deck—which
was very different from any part of the old
Sanda, for here everything was trim and
smart, the paint and varnish fresh and clean,
the brass-work as brilliant as polish could
make it. And Ogilvie fetched a deck-chair
for her, though she did not care to be seated ;
the run across to the North Quay would not
be of long duration.

He chatted pleasantly to her for a little
while, about the ordinary topics of Duntroone ; and Barbara did her best to answer
with animation and accord, though at times
she was a little hampered for want of the
proper English phrase. One thing she did

manage : she cured him of the habit of calling her " Miss Maclean."

" My name is Barbara," she said, almost with reproach.

" I'm sure I beg your pardon, Miss Barbara—I ought to have remembered—— "

" But how could you remember ? " said she, coyly ; " I am sure now you do not recollect where it was that we first met."

" Indeed, I do, then," he answered at once. " And the next time we meet on such an occasion, I will look to you to give me a dance."

" I hope so," murmured Barbara, with some touch of colour, and lowered eyes.

The train crept into the station ; and presently a few passengers made their appearance, coming towards the *Aros Castle.* Among the first of these to reach the gangway were a lady and her two daughters, the latter tall, fair-haired, English-looking girls, with good features and distinguished bearing. As the little stout mamma stepped on deck, she bestowed a brief nod of recognition upon the Purser, who respectfully raised his cap ; then she and her charges went below to the saloon, to deposit there their wraps and rugs and books.

"That is Mrs. Stewart of Innistroan," said Jack Ogilvie to Barbara, in a confidential whisper.

Almost immediately thereafter the three ladies reappeared; and the mother, coming over to where the Purser was standing, said—perhaps a trifle brusquely—

"Can I speak with you for a moment, Mr. Ogilvie?"

Barbara was thus left alone; but she could all the more carefully study the dress and bearing of these three new-comers, whom Ogilvie seemed to regard with considerable deference. Ordinarily he was rather off-hand in his manner; but now, in speaking to this Mrs. Stewart—probably about some business-matter—he was quite subdued and attentive. And as for the two girls, about whom Barbara was chiefly curious: she could not but be conscious of their air of distinction, however simply and plainly they might be dressed. Something, she knew not what, told her they were of " the gentry." With intense but concealed scrutiny she watched their demeanour as they listened to the Purser; she observed the half-indifferent look, the occasional glance towards the surrounding neighbourhood. As for their costume, it seemed to be the perfection of unostentatious neatness and fitness; the only ornament that each wore—so far as she could see—was an insignificant little brooch consisting of a ptarmigan's foot set in silver, that fastened the collar of the blue serge jacket.

But by this time the hawsers had been thrown off, and the *Aros Castle* was moving across to the other quay. Ogilvie came back to Barbara.

"This is a very short sail you have taken with us," he said to her, in his easy and familiar way, as they were approaching the pier. "Some other time you and Miss Jessie must go for a run with us to Tobermory, and there we will pick you up on our way back. I know that Mrs. Maclean has friends at Tobermory."

The steamer was now slowing; and it turned out that Barbara was the only passenger that meant to land. When the gangway had been shoved out, she timidly took her purse from her pocket—it was probably but poorly furnished.

"Will you tell me——" she said, bashfully, when he interrupted her: he had noticed that little movement.

" No, no ; no, no," said he, smiling, and
he put up his hand in a deprecatory fashion.
" You must not think of such a thing. We
shall only be too glad to take you across the
bay, any time you happen to be on the other
side. And tell Miss Jessie she must bring
you for a longer sail."

She said good-bye, and stepped ashore ;
she watched the passengers embark, and the
Aros Castle steam away again ; soon she lost
sight of Ogilvie, who had apparently gone
below ; and the last figures she could make
out were those of the two tall young ladies,
who had seemed to possess so strange and
mysterious a quality of attraction and perfection, even to the fancy of a girl.

When she went up into the town, she met
her cousin Jess, who had been along to buy
some wool ; and as they proceeded home
together, they encountered Lauchlan Mac-
Intyre. The shoemaker was of morose
aspect.

" You'll be coming to the lecture to-
morrow night, Mr. MacIntyre ? " said Jess,
pleasantly.

" I'm not so sure," responded Long
Lauchie, in melancholy tones. " It seems a
fearfu' waste of opportunity. To think of a

lecture on such things as songs, when there's but the one subject that is of tremendous concern to us, and that's the crying evil that is ruining us as a nation. Ay, just ruining us—ruining us—the curse of drink that is destroying the kintry from end to end. And what can we do, but wrestle with it, in Parliament and out of Parliament, in season and out of season, ay, and mek every election turn on it, and every candidate pledged for total abolition, ay, and have a section of the Rechabites in every fullage everywhere, until we put down and stamp out this terrible, terrible drink. There must be no peace until the whisky traffic is wholly rooted out ; and until a brand is put on a man that would be seen to enter a public-house—ay, a just persecution—a lawful persecution—there must be no moderation—no mercy—— "

" But you'll drive common-sense folk into rebellion," Jess said, good-humouredly. " Would you have them take to drink in self-defence ? "

" Aw, to hear you talk like that, and you at your years ! " said the shoemaker, almost in despair. " As sure's death it's just fearful to hear one of your years talk like that. And to think that you are on the side of

the drunkards, and the licensed victuallers,
and Sodom and Gomorrah.   But there's time
for ye yet.   If you'll tek a warning, ye may
turn yet.   You'll come over to us—ay—
you'll come over to us and be saved—as sure
as death, you'll be saved."

"Well, indeed, Mr. MacIntyre," said Jess
—and her pretty grey eyes, that at times
were rather inclined to sarcasm, were now
perfectly demure, "I'm not afflicted with any
great craving except now and again for a
cup of tea; but when the hour of trial comes
—when I have to fight the demon—it will
be a great thing for me to have an example
to look to.   And you'll give me a word of
encouragement——"

"I will, I will," said the shoemaker,
solemnly and sadly; and with that he continued on his way; while Jess turned to her
cousin Barbara, who had for some time been
staring into the window of the jeweller's
shop.

It was a favourite resort of hers.   For
here she could feast her eyes on treasures
that were far beyond her means—silver
fastening-pins set with lemon-yellow, and
white, and clear lilac cairngorms—scent-
bottles inlaid with the various clan tartans—

brooches, bracelets, necklets studded with
Iona stones—ear-rings, finger-rings, sleeve-
links, lockets—tray after tray of fascinating
nick-nacks of the very names of many of
which she was entirely ignorant. And at
this moment, when Jess said—

"Will you wait a moment, Barbara, or
will you come into the shop? I want Mr.
Boyd to see what is the matter with my
watch——"

—Barbara accepted the invitation with a
secret joy; though it was in a timorous kind
of fashion that she followed her cousin
into this magician's palace of wonders and
splendours. She looked all round the
jeweller's shop with an awe-stricken air;
and then her eyes came back to the glass
cases on the counter, where there was an
endless variety of surprisingly beautiful
objects. Not only that, but a tray of
brooches, that a customer had been inspecting
just before they came in, remained open on
the top of one of the cases; so that if she
chose she could take up any one of those
marvels for closer examination. And so
while Mr. Boyd—who was an old friend
of the Macleans, and a solicitous, kindly,
amiable sort of man—was inquiring into

the state and condition of Jessie's watch, Barbara was passing in review these priceless things, comparing and admiring and coveting. But in especial she was attracted by the brooch that occupied the place of honour in the middle of the tray. It was formed of a ptarmigan's foot, set in gold, with a deep yellow cairngorm above and another stone of the same kind and colour fixed in the middle claw. Now the ptarmigan brooches worn by the two young ladies who were on board the *Aros Castle*—and whom Jack Ogilvie seemed to treat with so much respect—were very plain and simple ornaments; here was something of a similar character, but more rich and resplendent, and better calculated for purposes of display. Alas! she knew too well that it was far away out of the reach of her small savings; such means and methods of drawing attention, of compelling admiration, were for people whose purses were abundantly filled.

Ultimately it was decided that the recusant watch should be left behind; and then, business over, Mr. Boyd proceeded to a little neighbourly gossip, in the course of which Barbara was introduced to him, her beautiful eyes winning favour as usual. The friendly jeweller sent his best regards to the widow; and finally Jessie and Barbara left the shop.

But they had gone only a few yards when Mr. Boyd came after them—he had not stayed to put on any kind of head-covering.

"Miss Maclean," said he, and simultaneously both girls turned. "I beg your pardon, but did you happen to notice a gold ptarmigan-brooch—it was in a tray on the counter——"

At the same moment there was a slight click as of something dropping on the pavement. He glanced downwards.

"Oh, here it is," he said; and he stooped and picked it up.

For a second there was silence. The watchmaker looked grave and troubled; Jess appeared to be astonished and perplexed rather than frightened; Barbara, timid as a fawn as she ordinarily was, alone remained perfectly impassive in countenance.

"It must have caught on to some part of your dress," said Mr. Boyd, slowly, and with some constraint. "Well, I'm sorry to have caused you any trouble." And thereupon and with no further word he returned to his shop.

But on the evening of this same day,

sitting by his fireside, John Boyd seemed thoughtful and depressed ; and his wife would insist on knowing the reason. And at last, under severe injunctions of secrecy, he revealed to her the story.

"I cannot tell what to think," he continued, as if communing with himself. "I made the excuse, then and there, for the sake of my old friend Mrs. Maclean. And maybe it was true : maybe their dress did catch up the brooch. Such things have happened. For how can I believe that Jessie Maclean, or this cousin of hers, that seems a nice, modest, quiet sort of a girl, would knowingly lift a piece of jewellery from the counter and carry it away ? I cannot believe it. And then, ye see, goodwife, I did not actually find it in the possession of either of them. If I had, it would have been my duty to have called in the police—— "

"John!" exclaimed his wife. "Have ye taken leave of your wits ? Ay, and if it was the half of your shop in question, would ye bring scandal and disgrace on the remaining years of an old friend ? No, no!—not for half the shop, or whole of the shop! I'm better acquainted with ye than ye are yourself, man ! And no doubt it was the tassels and bugles that the young girls are so fond of nowadays that catched on to the brooch— no doubt at all that was it!"

"Maybe so, Jean, maybe so," said the watchmaker, who seemed to have been quite unhinged and upset by this incident. "But mind, not one word to any living creature. That is my charge to ye. Not one single word about it to any living creature."

CHAPTER XVIII.

A LECTURE AND THEREAFTER.

IT wanted but an hour to the lecture, yet
Jess Maclean did not stir ; she sate silent and
absorbed—an unusual mood with her, for
she was naturally of a merry temperament ;
her head was bent over her needlework,
and she did not look up when she was
spoken to.

" Jess," said her mother, " what has ailed
you all the day long ? Anyone would think
this should be a great occasion for you—you
that has always been so proud of Allan
Henderson, and telling us what we might
expect of him. And now he is appearing
before the public—and a great many people
coming to see him—and who should be
more pleased than yourself—ay, and more to
the front at such a time, for Allan is never

tired of saying that you are the best friend and adviser he has got—— "

"I am not going to the lecture, mother," said Jess.

"Well, well, now, and what is the meaning of it all?" the widow demanded. She regarded her daughter a little more narrowly, and was alarmed to see that there were tears in her eyes. "What is the matter, Jess?" she exclaimed.

"What is the matter, mother?—what is the matter?" the girl cried, suddenly bursting into a passionate fit of weeping and sobbing. "How can I go to the lecture—how can I face those people—when I am a suspected thief?"

And there and then, in incoherent fashion, she told the story of the incident of the previous day, over which she had been brooding for four-and-twenty hours and more. Meanwhile the little widow's indignation was like to have altogether overcome her powers of utterance.

"And that's John Boyd—that's John Boyd!" she managed to say at last—though she was about breathless with anger and scorn. "And who but your own father was it that helped him when he had to make a composition with

his creditors over twenty years ago, ay,
helped to make him the well-to-do man he is
this day; and the best of friends we were
supposed to be; and now it's this John
Boyd—it's this John Boyd that comes forward
and accuses one of my girls of being a thief!"
She rose from her chair and threw aside her
work. "Well," said she, with resolute lips,
"this very minute I am going along to have
a word with John Boyd. I will see what
he means by calling either of my girls a
thief—— "

"Mother," interposed Jess, piteously, "he
did not say that—he did not say anything
of the kind. When he spoke it was to make
an excuse. It was Mr. Boyd himself that
suggested it was likely the brooch had caught
on to the dress of one or other of us. That's
what he said. But all the same I could see
what he was thinking. I saw his look—
though I did not quite understand it till
afterwards. And ever since I have been
going over what happened; and now—now
I know what he was thinking when he
picked up the brooch from the pavement. I
know it—I know it—I could see it—and—
and I never thought to be taken for a thief."
And here there was a fresh burst of crying.

"It isn't for a thief," she said, between her
sobs, "to go to hear Allan's lecture—and
face all those people—— "

"Jess," said Mrs. Maclean, firmly, "you'll
do as I bid ye. You'll go across to the
house, and get yourself dressed and ready,
and you'll put out my best things, and you'll
send Kirsty over to help me to shut up the
shop. I was not going to the lecture; but
now I am going; and I do not care who the
people are, but I will show them, when
Barbara and you go in, that you can hold
up your heads with any. And as for John
Boyd—— "

"Mother, you must not quarrel with Mr.
Boyd," pleaded Jess. "It was only natural
he should be startled. And he is an old
friend—— "

"Ay, and you do not know the saying,
then?" retorted the little widow, sharply,
"'Friendship is as it's kept.' The man that
suspects either you or Barbara of being a
thief is no friend of mine. But away with
ye, now, and get ready—if Barbara will let
you have five minutes of the looking-glass,
for she's a fearfu' creature for making much
of herself and decking herself up. And
when Mr. McFadyen comes, you will tell

him he must get me a ticket, and I will pay him for it afterwards."

Peter McFadyen was an important and a consequential man this night. The provost, who had consented to preside at the meeting, had been summoned away to Edinburgh on business connected with the town; and the senior councillor, nothing loth, had been prevailed on to take his place. And fully sensible of his responsibility was Peter. When the members of the Literary and Scientific Association, and their friends, with many of the towns-folk, and a few representatives of the neighbouring gentry, were at length assembled in the Masonic Hall, the chairman was in nowise facetious and droll— as if he were in Mrs. Maclean's back-parlour ; he was dignified, and measured of speech. And when, in formally introducing the lecturer to the audience, he had pronounced a pompous little eulogium, which caused Allan to look particularly uncomfortable, Mr. McFadyen thereafter glanced down towards the Macleans, who were seated in the front row, it was plain he would have said— 'Do you perceive that now ? A man may be sprightly and jocular enough in the freedom of private society, and yet know

how to perform his public duties with proper
state and decorum.' Alas! Jessie Maclean
never looked his way—paid no heed to him.
She was intently regarding Allan—she was
tremblingly anxious that he should betray no
nervousness—in her heart she was beseeching
this audience to be kind and attentive and
sympathetic. Barbara, who had adorned
herself with her most effective finery, kept
cevertly watching the door : the handsome
Purser had not yet put in an appearance—
perhaps the *Aros Castle* was late, perhaps he
had forgotten the half-implied promise.

Jess need not have been concerned. When
the young schoolmaster rose and placed the
sheets of his MS. on the stand before him,
there was not a trace of nervousness about
him ; he acknowledged, and barely acknowledged, the friendly reception accorded him ;
and at once, and in a business-like way, proceeded with his lecture—the main thesis of
which was to the effect that, if the German
people were to vanish from the face of the
earth, leaving only this invaluable collection
of Volkslieder, the philosopher of future
centuries could reconstruct the nation, with
all its desires, aims, habits, and occupations,
from these various and artless utterances.

But it was when he proceeded to give specimens of the folk-songs—using for the most part his own translations—songs of fiery patriotism, songs of plaintive home-yearning, love-songs and sad farewells, songs of simple family life, songs of banter and merriment, more rarely of sarcasm, joyous drinking songs, songs and choruses of the hunter's craft, legends and old-world tales—then it was that he captured the interest of his audience, and was rewarded by frequent if timid outbursts of applause. It was the non-literary ballad that he chose by pre-ference—the voice of the common people; but he could not well exclude Heine's 'Pilgrimage to Kevlaar,' or Uhland's 'Land-lady's Daughter,' for they also were of the people. And when he repeated a lover's passionate appeal to his sweetheart, or told some pathetic story of half-forgotten times, was he not really addressing, out of all this audience, only one? There was some com-parison of these German folk-songs with the Gaelic songs of the West Highlands, and mention made of one or two well-known favourites: all this was meant for Barbara—since she had been so graciously kind as to come to the lecture.

And yet it may be doubted whether Barbara heard anything more than an occasional word or phrase, conveying next to nothing. She had abandoned any hope she may have entertained of seeing Jack Ogilvie appear at the door of the hall; and now her attention was turned to the hall itself, the like of which she had never beheld before. For over the deep red walls hung a wonderful ceiling of clear grey-blue; and at the further end of the ceiling a golden sun sent out flashing rays, while at the other extreme shone a silver moon surrounded by seven stars. Then all round the room were mysterious devices; and there were painted pillars; and an arch; and in the keystone of the arch an eye that glared at her as if out of some vague immensity. Compass, square, and trowel she might or might not understand—they were commonplace emblems; but this immovable eye seemed to have some incomprehensible and compelling power of scrutiny; it fascinated her; she could not get away from that relentless gaze. And so, if she did listen at all, it was in a mechanical fashion. 'Prinz Eugen der edle Ritter,' 'Doctor Eisenbart,' 'Der Jäger aus Kurpfalz,' had apparently but little interest for her.

Nevertheless, something did at last happen
to arouse her from her apathetic dreaming.
The lecturer had been giving examples of
the better-known of the German bacchanalian
songs—'Crambambuli,' 'Im kühlen Keller,'
and the like—when, to everybody's amazement, a tall and gaunt form was seen to rise
in the very midst of the assemblage. It
was Long Lauchie, the shoemaker. For a
moment he seemed frightened at his own
temerity, and looked round in a helpless
way; but there was an inward monitor to
support him; the next second he had found
his speech.

"I am not wishing to interrupt," he said,
in Gaelic, "but every man has his duty,
and I will not stand by and be listening in
silence——"

"Order, order," called the chairman, with
a portentous frown.

But the shoemaker, pale as he was on
finding himself in this novel position, with
all eyes turned towards him, was not to be
deterred.

"It is I that must make my protest, if
there is to be such praise for drinking, and
not a word of warning to the young——"

"Order, order," the chairman called out

again; and then he added, with still greater severity : "MacIntyre, sit down, and behave yourself!"

Meanwhile the lecturer had stopped, and was calmly waiting to hear what Long Lauchie had to say. It was Mrs. Maclean who was most violently indignant over the interruption.

"That tipsymaniac!" she exclaimed, in an undertone. "Will nobody put him out? To bring disgrace on a meeting like this, and Allan going on just splendid!"

"Such praise of the sin of drinking," continued the shoemaker, doggedly, "I will set my face against, no matter how many there may be to cry me down. I have no word to say against the young man, Allan Henderson; it is not I that have a word to say against him; but when I hear such fearful things repeated, I am bound to lift up my voice. Yes, indeed. Is there anyone here that knows what drink is doing in this land —what terrible, terrible things are happening all through the whisky——?"

"Lauchlan MacIntyre," called out the chairman—who was beside himself with rage and shame on finding his authority thus scouted, "if you do not instantly resume

your seat, I will ask one or two of the young
men near you to remove you from this
assembly.   Do you hear me, now ? Will
you sit down ? "

" Drink," the shoemaker went on, " is the
ruin and curse of this country—it is bringing
a judgment upon us—— "

" Then I do call on the young men," broke
in Peter, with concealed fury. " Remove
him !   You there near him, remove that
person ! Put him out.   I, as chairman of
this meeting, authorise you to put him out."

Well, there were two or three of the
younger lads only too glad to have a little
bit of fun ; and the luckless shoemaker—
offering no physical resistance, it is true, but
still insisting on his conscientious protest
against anything that savoured of the praise
of drink—was haled away and conducted to
the door, and ejected into the night.   Thereafter peace and harmony were restored : and
the lecture was continued and ended in the
most satisfactory manner, a unanimous vote
of thanks to the schoolmaster bringing the
proceedings to a close.

And very lively and content was the little
supper-party that later on assembled at Mrs.
Maclean's—a supper-party limited to five, at

the cunning suggestion of the councillor. For, said he, they could be much merrier, with less of restraint, when they were ' by themselves ' ; and ' by themselves ' had come to mean himself and Jess, and Allan and Barbara, with the widow as hostess and guardian. This, therefore, was the circle now gathered round the hospitable board ; and a very happy little circle it seemed to be. Jess, in especial, was in great spirits ; she was delighted with the way everything had gone off, and at the reception accorded to her hero ; though, as usual, she could not help jibing and mocking at him.

"There's some that pretend to be very masterful, and cool, and undisturbed," said she, darkly. "But when I see a young man that is impatient of every word of intro-duction—though all kinds of fine things are being said about him—and that is anxious to plunge at once into the business before him, I can tell that he is just as timorous as a mouse, for all his affectation of com-posure."

"If you mean me, Jessie," said the school-master, laughing, "I will confess this to you, that I think I must have been nervous. I did not know it at the time ; but I guess that it must have been so, from the sensation of relief I have now that it's all over."

" I hope," observed Mr. McFadyen, who still preserved a certain air of state, " I hope I was not too severe in rebuking that fool of a man, MacIntyre—— "

" Severe!" cried the little widow, with returning indignation. " He should have been locked up by the police! To interrupt a meeting in that way! I declare it made me feel quite historical—I was like to choke——"

" And I trust there was no undue violence," continued the councillor, still with something of a grand air, " on the part of the young men who removed him. It was a painful duty that devolved upon me; but I had to execute it; and I trust there was no undue violence——"

" Oh, you need not trouble about that, Mr. McFadyen," Jess said, blithely. " The young lads who carried out your orders—and the shoemaker—did it as peaceably as was possible."

" Ah, well, ah, well," said Peter, with a sigh of satisfaction, " it was but a trifling incident, after all; and one may fairly say that the whole evening was a distinct success.

And though in a measure I was responsible for the conduct of the proceedings, still, I do not think I am taking credit to myself when I maintain that everything went off just beautiful. And, mind you, Allan, lad, it's a great thing for you to keep yourself before the public—you that's starting the Latin class, and having a fine career before ye, as we all of us hope. It's a great thing to be known and respected by your fellow-townsmen; and I was well pleased to see, when ye stood up, that ye had a friendly welcome from them—— "

"And what did you think of the Masonic Hall, Miss Barbara?" said the young schoolmaster, turning abruptly to his neighbour—for he did not like this talk about himself.

"I was never seeing any place like that before," the girl said. "And I could not understand the meaning of the things on the walls. There was one, in front of me, that was very strange—it looked like a large eye, single and staring—— "

"Oh, that is the All-seeing Eye—I suppose, for I am not a mason," he said.

She regarded him for a moment doubtfully.

"All-seeing?" she repeated; and then she

said, with some petulance : " But how can it be All-seeing, when it is only painted on the wall ? "

" It is merely an emblem," he replied, with great gentleness. " It does not pretend to be anything but a symbol—— "

" Is it put there to frighten people ? " she demanded, resentfully.

" Why, surely not ! "

" Then what is the use of it ?—though anyone knows that an eye painted on a wall cannot be seeing anything ! " she said. And this was her last word on the subject; and sufficiently enigmatic it was; for he knew nothing of what secret imaginings had been passing through her mind, as she sate and half-listened to the discourse about German folk-songs.

Altogether, a cheerful and pleasant hour or so, after the serious labours of the evening were over; but it was growing late; and at length Mr. McFadyen and Allan rose to go. Nevertheless, the councillor was still loquacious; for there was to be a great match at golf between the station-master and himself, on the following Monday afternoon; and he was anxious that Jessie, and Barbara, and Mrs. Maclean, too, if that were possible, should witness the contest; and he was discussing this project as he went to the door, both Jess and her mother accompanying him. This was Allan's opportunity—Barbara having remained behind: it was an opportunity thrust upon him, as it were chance-wise—an opportunity he could not, and did not care to, avoid. For he was in a perturbed and reckless mood; the events of the evening had in some measure excited him; still more so the bewilderment of having once again been sitting next this beautiful creature, with glimpses of the raven-black tangles of her hair, and an occasional glance from the deep, clear, mystic eyes. And now, when the others had gone on, he turned to her; she became aware of his approach; a sudden touch of apprehension appeared in her face.

"Barbara," he said—and his tones were low and impassioned, "is it too soon for me to speak?"

She uttered no word—she looked afraid.

"Did you hear what some of those lovers said in the songs?" he went on. "And did you not take it to yourself—as if I were appealing to you? For—for surely you understand. You came to me out of the night and the dark; and now I want you to go with me through the long day—the long day that I hope lies before us two together. Will you do that, Barbara? Or is it too soon to ask?"

"Yes, yes," she said, with quick relief, "it is that——it is too soon yet——"

"But only too soon?" he urged, seeking in vain for some answering message from those downcast eyes. "Later on, when you have got used to thinking of it, you will not fear to say yes—you will let me hope for that?"

But again she was silent; and here were Jess and her mother returning from the outer staircase; so that for the present there was no assurance for him—only the solace that now she knew what lay in his mind, burning there like a consuming fire.

END OF VOL. I.

LONDON: PRINTED BY WILLIAM CLOWES AND SONS, LIMITED,
STAMFORD STREET AND CHARING CROSS.